Elijah Robinson Kennedy

John B. Woodward

A Biographical Memoir

JOHN B. WOODWARD

A BIOGRAPHICAL MEMOIR

BY

ELIJAH R. KENNEDY

❦

FOR PRIVATE DISTRIBUTION

❦

NEW-YORK
PRINTED AT THE DE VINNE PRESS
MDCCCXCVII

Elijah Robinson Kennedy

John B. Woodward
A Biographical Memoir

ISBN/EAN: 9783337031350

Printed in Europe, USA, Canada, Australia, Japan

Cover: Foto ©Raphael Reischuk / pixelio.de

More available books at **www.hansebooks.com**

PREFACE

Being asked by General Woodward's brother to prepare a memoir of the General, and understanding that it was the desire of the family, I undertook the task, regretting, however, that I was not better qualified to adequately portray the amiable and notable character of my friend.

Especial acknowledgment is due to General George W. Wingate for assistance in the narrative of General Woodward's military service. Professor Franklin W. Hooper is entitled to thanks for collating the facts of General Woodward's association with the Brooklyn Institute.

E. R. K.

Brooklyn, May, 1897.

CONTENTS

LIFE OF JOHN B. WOODWARD

I

ANCESTRY AND EARLY LIFE

JOHN BLACKBURNE WOODWARD was born in Brooklyn on the thirty-first day of May, 1835. His ancestors were of Shakespeare's county. His great-great-grandfather Isaac Woodward, born about the last year of the seventeenth century, was a farmer in the parish of Berkswell, Warwickshire, where, and in neighboring parishes, the family had been known for many generations. Rugby and Leamington, Guy's Cliff, Stoneleigh Abbey, Warwick Castle, the imposing ruins of Kenilworth, and the romantic haunts around Stratford-on-Avon were all within easy distances of "Marsh Farm." The battle-ground of Naseby was not too remote for a day's excursion, and the "three tall spires of Coventry" were but little more than five miles distant. On the

death of Isaac Woodward his oldest son, also
named Isaac, succeeded to the farm, and when
he too was gathered to his fathers the property passed to the control of his oldest son,
whose name was Thomas. The Woodwards
were thrifty. Thomas prospered so that after
a few years he left the place he had inherited
and took a larger place at Wotton Green, in
the same parish. In 1789 he married Martha
Buckerfield, the daughter of a Quaker trades-
man of Kenilworth. Of the children of this
union, the third, Thomas, was the father of
John B. Woodward.

During the Napoleonic wars the farmers
of England throve beyond all precedent.
"Wheat rose to famine prices," says the his-
torian of the English People, "and the value
of land rose in proportion with the price of
wheat." Thomas Woodward, senior, and his
sons were cultivating the farm at Wotton
Green, investing their profits mainly in im-
provements and betterments; but the great
increase in the value of the place aroused the
greed of the landlord, who, taking advantage
of a defect in the lease due to his own failure

to sign that paper, demanded such a heavy advance in the rent that the Woodwards refused to pay and chose to give up their home, although that resulted in the abandonment of the greater part of all their property. They met their adversity with fortitude. The sons were apprenticed to various trades, and the father soon found employment in an iron foundry. Evidently his spirit was not crushed, and he was not content to settle into the ranks of ordinary workmen, for he invented several agricultural implements, the most important of which was an iron plow, believed to be the first ever made. Subsequently he moved to London and engaged in manufacturing. Although he succeeded fairly well, the times were extremely discouraging. All currents of trade and industry were disturbed while the country was adjusting its affairs to peace conditions after the long, feverish period of the Napoleonic and American wars, and business prospects were gloomy. The war with the United States directed renewed attention to the young republic, and after peace was established many adventurous Englishmen crossed over to seek

their fortunes in the new world. Perhaps the
best known of these was William Cobbett.
His writings on public questions had enjoyed
a large circulation, and his imprisonment for
the force and freedom of his utterances in
popular causes had raised him to a position of
great influence. He was hopeless of the future of the old country. After traveling in
America he sent back glowing accounts of the
States. In one of his letters, written from his
farm on Long Island for publication in England, he said, " Worried, my old neighbors, as
you are, by tax-gatherers of all descriptions,
from the County Collector, who rides in his
coach and four, down to the petty Window
Peeper, the little miserable spy who is constantly on the lookout for you, as if you were
thieves; surrounded as you are by this ver-
min, big and little, you will with difficulty
form an idea of the state of America in this
respect. It is a state of such blessings, when
compared with the state of things in England,
that I despair of being able to make you fully
understand what it is."

The business of the Woodwards was now

established in London and certainly was not unprosperous, but the father was a reader of Cobbett, whose writings excited in the mind of the disciple great hope that he might better his fortunes in America. Accordingly in the spring of 1818 his son, Thomas Woodward, Jr., was sent to America to look the ground over. The reports he made were of such an encouraging nature that late in the same year the father with his entire family started for New York, where they arrived early in the following year.[1]

Thomas Woodward's first wife died in 1804, but he had married again, and the family he brought to America consisted of his wife and his four sons. Directly after they were settled here Thomas Woodward, Jr., learned the silversmith's trade and soon formed a partnership with his brothers Charles and George and a Mr. Hale. Later Mr. Hale retired and the business was continued under the firm name of

[1] In America the Woodward and Cobbett families became friends, and in 1871 J. P. Cobbett, a grandson of the publicist, presented to John B. Woodward a case of razors, which, as shown by an inscription, had been presented to William Cobbett by the city of Sheffield in 1830.

Woodward & Brothers for nearly forty years.
Originally it consisted of the manufacture of
pencils, but Thomas Woodward, who evidently
inherited his father's talent, made a number of
useful inventions, the most profitable of which
were the "Diamond Pointed Gold Pen," the
"Ever Pointed Pencil," and the "Shielded
Safety Pin." In 1828 he married Mary Barrow
Blackburne, daughter of John Blackburne and
Elizabeth Cook, who had emigrated from
Liverpool in 1822. Through her father, Captain Robins Cook, Mrs. Woodward was related
to Captain Cook the celebrated navigator.
The couple lived in New York City until 1829
or 1830, when they moved to Brooklyn. In
1832 Mr. Woodward built the house now
known as No. 100 Sands Street, numbered 84
at that time, where he resided until his decease
in 1873. There were four daughters born to
them and four sons, of whom John was the
oldest. When eight years old he was sent to
school to a man whom in later years he char-
acterized as "an irascible Irish pedagogue
named Williams." This Williams has been
described as good hearted and quick tempered.

His impulsiveness got into his discipline more than the parents approved, and they determined to remove their son from his care. Public schools had not then been established, so the lad was tranferred to a private school kept by Miss Seaver in Classical Hall, Washington Street, the building recently used as headquarters by the Salvation Army. When ready for a higher grade young Woodward attended the school of Samuel Putnam. Long afterward the pupil spoke of this teacher as "a scholar, a gentleman, and a thorough pedagogue." From here the boy was promoted to the academy of Benjamin W. Dwight, in Livingston Street between Clinton Street and Sidney Place. These were the best educational institutions of that period, and young Woodward made all possible use of their advantages until his fifteenth year, when he found employment in the office of his uncle George Woodward, an importer, in New York City. In 1859 Edward Haynes, an exporter of American products to the countries watered by the Rio de la Plata, invited the young man into his service on terms so encouraging that they were promptly accepted. His intelligence and zeal brought him early promotion and it was not long before he was managing the entire concern. Indeed, the young clerk evinced such decided talents and such trustworthiness that he was soon taken into partnership. On the first of January, 1881, Mr. Haynes having retired on account of broken health, General Woodward became sole proprietor, and thus he remained until his decease. His relations with merchants in South America ripened into warm friendships which were severed only by his death.

That he possessed unusual business ability is evidenced by the prosperous management of his own concern and by his success in restoring to sound conditions companies and institutions that were put in his charge when they were on the verge of bankruptcy. An extensive manufacturing establishment, having become seriously embarrassed, was soon reorganized by him and became more profitable than it had been previously or has been since. A large financial institution fell into an unprosperous state and its capital was impaired.

General Woodward took the presidency, brought strong men and new elements into the directorate, and in a couple of years turned the institution over to a successor, thoroughly rehabilitated. In trust companies, insurance companies, and other organizations with which he was associated, his energy was of great service, his wisdom in council was highly prized, and his imperturbable good nature often reconciled conflicting elements and established harmony. And yet he acquired much less fortune than many men of smaller capacity and less favorable opportunities. The explanation is not far to seek. It is not that he was charitable and generous—that he surely was—but General Woodward gave up to the unremunerated service of others and the public so much of his time, and such a share of his thought and ability and enthusiasm, that others and the public were the chief beneficiaries of his talents and labors. He lacked only the will to turn his first-rate abilities to selfish uses to have become a very rich man, but because of that lack he left a far more precious legacy than "great riches."

2

His readiness to serve others was inborn and was observed while he was yet a lad. It continued through his entire life and was perhaps the cause of his untimely death. He was a truthful man, a devoted son, a loving brother, a fond husband and father, a genial and loyal friend, an able administrator, a successful military commander, a public-spirited citizen, and in every relation in life his most conspicuous characteristic was usefulness. This trait, displayed through his entire career, and in an unusual degree, enabled him to be of great service to his family and to many relatives and friends, to commercial enterprises, to philanthropy in practical operation, to the cause of religion, to liberal and elegant culture, to fraternity among men, to civil government, to the military system of his state, and to the nation in its supreme crisis. No one knows, and it is impossible to estimate, the number of individuals to whom he rendered help of one sort or another. A comparatively late instance is that of a sculptor, now become eminent, whose fame was greatly augmented by a superb work for which he per-

haps never would have received the order if
General Woodward had not vouched so thoroughly for his fitness and backed up his
voucher by giving his bond for fifty thousand
dollars warranting that the young artist
should complete the commission within the
time stipulated and according to the accepted
design.

General Woodward's first public service was
in the volunteer fire department, which at the
time occupied a peculiar and interesting relation to municipal affairs and to society.
When he was perhaps only seventeen years
old he joined a hose company. He did not remain long in the department, but the period
was sufficient to prove that he had moral
stamina enough to resist temptations that led
to the ruin of several young fellows who were
his associates. Some of his experiences in the
department he used in after years to relate
with hearty merriment. One was of an occasion when, being at the moment of an alarm
near the house where the hose carriage was
kept, he "took the tongue" with another
member of the company. While drawing the

carriage out they were joined by still another member and the three started down Fulton Street, near Sands Street, where the grade is very steep. The man who had hold of the rope soon let go and sought safety on the sidewalk. Shortly after the man on the other side of the tongue was compelled to relinquish his grip; but the General's legs, which he described as making the longest and fastest strides they ever had made or were capable of making, enabled him to continue for some time steering the machine alone. At last the pace grew too hot even for him and he let go, but the hose carriage continued running, and its momentum was so great that it went straight on and over into the river. Forty years after he would tell this with bated breath lest the enraged members of the old company should discover who was the culprit responsible for this inglorious accident to their pet machine. While such incidents and the association with firemen were exciting, he nevertheless soon discovered that his tastes led in another direction, so he resigned from the hose company and thus left the fire department.

II

ENLISTMENT IN THE MILITIA AND SERVICE
UNDER PRESIDENT LINCOLN'S FIRST
CALL FOR TROOPS

ON the twenty-third of June, 1854, when
he was nineteen years of age, young
Woodward joined the "Brooklyn City Guard,"
afterward Company G, Thirteenth Regiment
New York State Militia. With brief intermis-
sions he continued in the service twenty-five
years, during which period he rose to the
highest position in the force. On the fifth of
October, 1855, he was made a Corporal and
on the third of April, 1857, First Sergeant.
On the eighteenth of February, 1861, he was
elected Second Lieutenant. In every place
he made an honorable reputation, and even
as "Orderly Sergeant Woodward" he won
considerable distinction.

The breaking out of the rebellion put the

national capital in imminent danger. The
President appealed to the loyal North for
troops and the National Guard organizations
were ordered to the front. Baltimore, which
commanded the communications between
Washington and the North, was at that time
controlled by rebel sympathizers, and the first
troops that marched through the city were
attacked and several of them were shot down
in the streets. Orders for the New York
militia to proceed to the front were issued
Thursday, the eighteenth of April, 1861, and
on the following Tuesday the Thirteenth
Regiment marched, six hundred strong. Not
only was nearly every member of the regiment in his place, but a large number of
new enlistments had been received. The
streets through which the regiment passed
were crowded with patriotic citizens the roar
of whose cheers made it almost impossible to
hear an order. Thirty-four years after, when
General Woodward, at the request of the Editor of the "New York Herald," recalled the circumstances, he said: "I was then Second Lieutenant of the Brooklyn City Guard, a company

armed as infantry and attached to the Thirteenth Regiment as Company G, commanded by Captain R. V. W. Thorne, Jr., who was educated at West Point and was a typical old army officer, a courteous gentleman in every sense of the word. As the outbreak had been foreseen by him he had worked to get the company in the best possible shape as regards organization and equipment, so that when the summons came his command was ready, and very few companies in the National Guard proved better prepared. The morning of the twenty-third of April found a full company, every office filled and every man equipped for active service. More than this, there was a waiting-list of over fifty whose joining at once followed upon the national uprising, who could not be got ready in time to leave with us, but they followed within a week or ten days. Their accession made the company one hundred and fifty strong, probably the largest company mustered into service under the first call of the President. . . . . . . As to the company itself, no finer, truer, better men were ever mustered into any service. I cannot now call the roll, but many of the names come back to my recollection. Of the officers, there were Evan M. Johnson, Jr., later on Controller of Brooklyn; John W. Elwell, afterward Lieutenant-Colonel of the Twenty-third Regiment; Samuel H. Kissam, a brother of Mrs. William H. Vanderbilt; Benjamin Haskell, Major, and Inspector of the Fifth Brigade; Drummer Edward G. McIntyre, now the famous Drum-Major of the Thirteenth Regiment; W. H. Bulkley, since then a general officer, and later Lieutenant-Governor of Connecticut; Morgan G. Bulkley, since Governor of Connecticut; Samuel W. Boocock, the trusted broker of Wall Street's greatest operators; William Barnett, afterward Captain of the company; Ned Bullock, now gone over to the silent majority, but whom all recall with affection; W. Henry Condit, who became the trusted agent in China of A. A. Low & Brother; John A. Cross, Jr., son of one of Brooklyn's early mayors; George R. Dutton, a New Jersey judge; Elbert H. Fordham, who afterward commanded one of Massachusetts' famous volunteer regiments; William A. Hunter, son of another Brooklyn mayor, and William R. Hunter, his cousin, who succeeded to the command of the company; Isaac Harris Hooper, who commanded the Fifteenth Regiment Massachusetts Volunteers at its muster out; Benjamin Kimberly, who earned fame as an officer of the Forty-fourth New York; Joe Leggett, known to every old Brooklynite as a ball player and volunteer fireman; Edwin W. Ludlam, now one of Brooklyn's gas magnates; Fred A. Mason, later a Colonel of the Thirteenth; Willis L. Ogden, recently Lieutenant-Colonel of the Twenty-third Regiment; Sam Patchen, gone on before—he was one of the noted family of that name, identified for years with Brooklyn's progress; Edwin B. Spooner, Jr., son of Brooklyn's first editor, himself an officer in the Forty-eighth New York Volunteers; Nelson A. Shaurman, before the war a captain of police, during the war Colonel of Brooklyn's Ninetieth Regiment, and Brigadier-General; Arthur Sherman, cashier of a great national bank; Clarence Stanley, ("Cupid"), afterward Adjutant; Robert B. Woodward, Adjutant and division staff officer; Harrison

3

White, of the Ira Harris Light Cavalry. These
scenes of the twenty-third of April come back
to me — the names of these comrades come
back out of the mists of thirty-four years. I
will let others recall the deeds of the famous
old 'mother of regiments,' my cherished Thirteenth."

The regiment proceeded by water to Annapolis, where it remained several weeks,
forming part of the command of General
Benjamin F. Butler. During this part of its
service it was in a number of scouting and
reconnoitering expeditions. In the meantime
General Butler made a descent upon Baltimore and seized the strong points in and
about the city, which he fortified and garri-
soned by the regiments under his command,
thus frustrating the purpose of the Southern
sympathizers to swing the place into line with
the rebel government. The Union forces were,
however, considered insufficient, and on the
sixteenth of June the Thirteenth Regiment
was sent to reinforce them, and here it remained during the balance of the term for
which it had enlisted. During the time the

regiment was away from home the young soldier wrote a number of letters which gave a lucid account of the campaign and conveyed vivid pictures of camp life. The letters are so characteristic of the man as he was at that time that it would interest his friends to publish them in full, but the limitations of this volume make it practicable to use only such passages as relate his own experiences.

The first letter is dated the twenty-fifth of April, 1861, on board the steamship *Marion*, in Chesapeake Bay, and is addressed to his father:

To set your mind at rest let me first tell you that we are all well and as jolly as if we had severally imbibed the spirit of Mark Tapley. We think we all deserve credit for being jolly, for until we got into this bay you never saw such a collection of woe-begone looking men in your life. Although we are well adapted for soldiers we make the worst kind of sailors. Hardly half a dozen of our company escaped without a sight of "swallows homeward flying." Fortunately the Twenty-eighth Regi-

ment were unable to get ready in time to take
this steamer, as was intended, or we should
have been unbearably crowded. As it is there
is hardly room to walk about on deck. The
officers are all very comfortably quartered in
state-rooms, but the privates are compelled to
sleep wherever they can find room on deck or
in the hold. Bob [his brother Robert B. W.]
was very uncomfortable the first night, as he
was sick and was obliged to lie on the open
deck. Last night I got him a place under the
dining-table in the saloon. I gave my berth
to Dick Lawrence, who was fearfully sick, and
I took my blanket and the floor. My hips
feel the effect this morning. The only incident, so far, of a warlike nature has been the
firing of a shot across the bows of a brig
which had not her colors flying. The Stars
and Stripes were run up in double quick time.
We are bound, as near as I can judge, to Annapolis, and thence for a tramp of thirty-five
miles to Washington. We are all much more
sanguine of a peaceful passage, as the steamer
Keystone State has just passed us and announced the presence of the Rhode Island

militia at Annapolis and the safe arrival of the Seventh Regiment of New York in Washington. Another vessel has informed us that the light-houses in this neighborhood have been destroyed. . . . If you see a report that Jno. B. W. is promoted to be First Lieutenant believe it, for it is true. If other promotions follow me as quickly I shall soon be in command of the U. S. Army.

The next letter is as follows:

DREAMING OF HOME, ANNAPOLIS, MD.
April 26th, 1861.

DEAR FATHER,

We have recovered from the effects of sea-sickness and feel quite soldierly again. If again compelled to go to war I hope they won't send me by sea. We arrived at this place last night at nine o'clock and anchored in the stream. At ten o'clock this morning we were brought ashore and landed at the grounds of the United States Naval Academy. Our company is quartered in three of the recitation rooms, each of which is about twenty feet square, the floor being covered with manilla matting. The boys are quite delighted with the luxurious sleeping-places provided them, for two nights' bunking on the deck of a steamer has quite changed their idea of what is essential to comfort. The officers are in one of the residences of the professors, but the rooms are entirely destitute of furniture, and I presume that the pine flooring and my hip bones will be in too close association to-night for me to be very comfortable. Our boys are so delighted with this place that they express a strong desire to remain the balance of their lives. . . . News has just reached us that the election for state convention in Maryland has resulted in the choice of Secessionists, so we look for squally times. I cannot yet reconcile myself to the idea that we are on a war expedition. We all feel so full of joke and heart that we forget we have pistols at our waists and boxes filled with ball cartridges.

The next letter is from Annapolis, and is dated the twenty-eighth of April:

I find that the duties of First Lieutenant are as much in advance of my expectation as is the pay. I therefore find it impossible to devote much time to writing letters. Rest assured I will omit no opportunity of communicating anything of importance to you, as I am sure you must be even more anxious to hear from us than we can be to hear from home, because we know you to be safe, except from the natural evils of life, whilst we are exposed to very great danger. We know this and will not fail in our duty to you any more than in our duty to our country.

I attended church to-day and listened to a splendid, although exceedingly pathetic, address of the chaplain of this post, who has to-day received what he termed a traitor's letter from his own son, who has taken up arms against his father and enlisted in the Southern army. It brought out all the finer feelings of the men. If you saw our departure you must have noticed the red-shirted company in our regiment [a company composed of members of the volunteer fire department]. You should, to appreciate these men, have seen the tears

roll down their faces.   You would think them
a hard class of men to get along with, but our
intercourse with them is as pleasant as with
any of the corps.

The next letter is from Annapolis, under
date of May second.

Monday I was despatched to Washington—
was highly delighted at having such an opportunity.   I went there by the railroad, which is
now in the possession of the government, the
entire road being guarded by the Sixty-ninth
Regiment, who have been stationed every few
hundred feet.   The capitol looks more like a
flour warehouse than a building for legislative
chambers.   The Seventh New York and most
of the Massachusetts regiments are quartered
there, besides fifteen thousand barrels of flour
on storage.   All the department buildings are
also converted into barracks. . . . . I was introduced by Lieutenant Mears, U. S. A., to
Secretary Cameron, who said that if I wished
to enter the army he thought it could be ar-
ranged.   I did not accept or decline it, as I

wished to hear from you. As I presume you would not like it I have not allowed myself to think much of taking it. My present pay as First Lieutenant is about $1600, (provided I get it), and the duties here suit me to death. The work is hard, as our recruits require much patience and about five hours' hard work a day. My voice is getting into pretty good training, and I have it so much under control as not to hurt me a particle. My recruits now drill as well as any old soldiers on the Point. I am getting a first-rate reputation as drill master and the members of our company will do anything for me. . . . . .

We have not a sick man on our list. All eat, work, and sleep well. Night is the funniest part of our time, as fifty of us sleep in one room, on the floor, and the noise from the heavy breathing and snoring is most comical. Hope Uncle Sam won't keep us much longer without our letters.

ANNAPOLIS, May 3d, 1861.

DEAR FATHER,

Fifteen minutes ago (9 P. M.) our quarters were tremendously excited by the arrival of

4

the mail. Most of our boys received letters,
and a jollier set it would be hard to find than
are now surrounding me. Am delighted to
hear from home, and to-morrow morning shall
start with new ardor for my work. All you
say will have strict attention. . . . . Four
of our men are detailed to escort Major Ander-
son to Washington to-morrow morning. This
order has just arrived and has stirred the
boys up higher than before. I read them that
you were at the drill every evening. The announcement was received with a regular tu-
mult of applause. When the detachment ar-
rives we shall have the largest company that
has left New York for the war. We have now
seventy-eight rank and file, and we see by the
papers that fifty-seven will follow, making a
total of one hundred and thirty-five. As the
law allows only one hundred men to the company it may be necessary to make two commands, in which case a further promotion
may await me. We prefer to keep one company and merely parade as two commands.
Everything remains quiet and orderly here.
I pass out frequently into the city, alone and

unattended, day and night, (attended a Masonic meeting once), and have never been treated differently from what I would have been in Brooklyn. The citizens have since our stay here much changed in opinion, and every day spreads a new lot of the Stars and Stripes to the breeze. The city appears to have been deserted by the wealthy, as the best houses are all closed. There seems to be very little business done, and yet few, if any, loafers. Those who remain here are workers.

The Fire Zouaves passed through this place this morning. They are the only troops that have been here who were unruly. I was standing near an old woman's pie stand when some of the Zouaves came up and asked the woman the price. She told them a levy apiece. The spokesman said, "Say, fellows, here's pies at a levy apiece. Let's levy on them." They followed his suggestion, and over went the old woman, and her pies were speedily stowed away. A few of us made the victim of the prank, (a negro, of course), square and passed on.

ANNAPOLIS, May 9th, 1861.

To-day the correspondence has quite rolled in on me, one letter having with it a parcel of cakes and sausages (from Lizzie, of course). . .

. . . Have finally dismissed the army position. My errand to Washington was double—apparently to take charge of some camp equipage for the Seventh Regiment, really to deliver important despatches to the War Department. This was not known even to the men who accompanied me, and I have not before this told any one. I was as glad to give up those despatches as was Sinbad the Sailor to get rid of the Old Man of the Mountain. If I did not deem my duty to my company paramount I should be frequently sent, as both General Butler and Colonel Smith apparently regard me with favor; but I am specially needed here whilst the recruits are raw. . . . . Evan Johnson to-day returns to the corps, we having waived our rights. To enable him to do this I have resigned the First Lieutenancy and am again Second Lieutenant; so I am promoted downward. The men grumble at me for my good nature, but I deem my action right. . . . . The piece of poetry from Lizzie I read aloud to the men. I think it the best of her composition I have read. I did not tell the men who wrote it, and there was great curiosity as to who the "only brothers" could be. None guessed right. I afterward told them.

The next letter was evidently written with some pride, for at the head there is a hand pointing to the significant letters "U. S. A." It is dated,

QUARTERS CO. G, THIRTEENTH REGIMENT, U. S. A.,

May 14th, 1861.

. . . . . I must not omit to mention that yesterday at 4 P. M. we, (our company only), were mustered into the United States service for three months from April 23d. The balance of the regiment will probably be sworn in in a few days. Company G, you see, is still ahead. Captain Thorne deserves more praise than can be told for the exertion he has made, ever since we first received orders, to place and keep us ahead. So well has he succeeded that

we daily refuse scores of the regiment who
wish to be transferred to our company. Besides, he is the most popular man, either on
the ground or in the city, connected with the
regiment. It is glory enough to serve under
such a man. . . . . . This afternoon we are ordered to parade for the purpose of marching
through the city, to celebrate the opening of
the railroad which our engineers have built
connecting our yard with the former depot of
the road. We regard the work as quite an
achievement, and are very proud of it.

The next letter begins with a memorandum
before the date, as follows:

I have done a little toward endorsing the
Stars and Stripes O. K.

The date is the eighteenth of May.

DEAR FATHER,

I have this moment (11 A. M.) returned from
the expedition upon which I was despatched
on the 16th instant.

The mission upon which we were sent was

to recapture a light-ship which was taken by the Secessionists from Smith's Point and stowed snugly away in a small creek about the width of Byron River, named Mill Creek, which empties into the Great Wycomico River, a tributary of this great bay. We arrived at the river at 5 A. M. yesterday, found out, by scaring a darky until his wool was white, where our prize lay, went there, saw her, got alongside of her, hitched on, and brought her here. The banks of the creek were high, looking as if washed away by the river, with underbrush to the very edges. From this the Lancaster Grays, who had charge of the ship, gave us a pretty warm fire. After patiently waiting a minute or two I gave the men orders to return it, which they did most gallantly. We cannot say whether we wounded or killed any, but I can say that not one of my men was touched, even in his clothes. This is miraculous, as we were exposed on the upper deck of one of the canal propellers without a particle of protection, unless the smoke-pipe may be considered one. Not a man flinched, and, with one exception, they watched my eye

and did not fire or move a muscle until ordered. In the instant of firing, by order of
Captain Flusser, U. S. Navy, (who commanded
the expedition), I had the American flag
raised. The three men designated for that
duty laid down their pieces and hoisted the
banner beautifully. We gave it three cheers
and went at it again. Our boys are much
pleased with their trip. Several articles will
be put in print about this, the first firing in
Virginia. I have no doubt they will draw it
pretty steep, so make a discount on what they
write. By a singular coincidence the propeller upon which we were is named the William
Woodward. I enclose a list of the men who
were with me. I have written in a hurry and
of course in some little excitement, as all the
men are still cheering or talking around me.
The ink used I found on board the prize, and
have written you the first account of our success from that bottle.

Yours affectionately,

Jno. B. Woodward, *Lieut. U. S. A.*

P. S. I forgot to mention that returning we
overhauled a schooner, which turned out all

right, and we were in turn overhauled by a government vessel which cruises off the Potomac. The latter incident made much excitement, as we feared, on her approach, that she might be a Secessionist vessel ordered to recapture our prize.

The list of names in the detachment follows, and as this was, as Lieutenant Woodward states, the first firing in Virginia, and an event, therefore, of unique interest, they are given here:

Lieutenant WOODWARD, in command.

Sergeants.	*Corporals.*
KISSAM and ECHALAZ.	HYDE and COOMBS.

Privates.

1	FULLER, 1st	9	LORD
2	FULLER, 2d	10	PLUMMER
3	STRACHAN	11	THOMÆ
4	SHAURMAN	12	BOOCOCK
5	PATCHEN	13	DANA
6	YOUNG	14	TITUS (ALFRED)
7	WALDEN (C. C.)	15	HOOPER
8	MORE	16	McCOBB

Privates. — (Continued.)

17	LAWRENCE	35	SHEFFIELD
18	WOODWARD (R. B.)	36	WHITNEY
19	WHEELWRIGHT	37	WILSON
20	SMITH (G. H.)	38	BULKELEY (W. H.)
21	WILLARD	39	CONDIT
22	HITCHCOCK	40	HOPKINS
23	KIMBERLEY	41	BULLOCK
24	ERKENBRECK	42	HARPER
25	McFARLAN	43	HAYNES (TIM)
26	PLACE	44	WHITE (G. B.)
27	STANLEY	45	FORDHAM
28	BEST	46	SPENSE
29	DUCKWITZ	47	WALSH
30	ROCHE	48	CROSS
31	ROYCE	49	ROBINSON
32	AYERS	50	SMITH (CAD.)
33	RIDNER	51	BARNET
34	TAYLOR (S. C.)		Total . . . 56.

The rebel account of this affair, taken from a Southern paper, is curious reading. The information was furnished, so the paper said, "by Lucian Hall of the Lancaster (Va.) Grays."

"It is untrue that any of our 'rebels' were killed in the recent skirmish in the recapture of the Smith's Point light-ship. On the other hand some eight or ten Federal troops must have been killed and a number wounded. A man at the masthead was struck by a minié ball and fell with great violence to the deck. His fellow troops instantly gathered around in great numbers, and, taking advantage of the moment, our volunteers let fly another volley at the bunch. Several fell under the fire. About this time the Federal troops became highly exasperated and returned the fire with much spirit. Mysterious as it may seem, not a man on our side was hurt. The boat now hurried off as quickly as possible, and not until she was beyond the range of musket-balls did the volunteers cease to fire upon them. In passing out of the Wycomico River the propeller stopped a small vessel and took possession of the captain, but subsequently let him go. The captain states that the decks were partially covered with blood. He innocently inquired of an officer how many were killed. 'That 's none of your d—— busi-

ness,' was the reply. The inference was plain
that somebody was. This is authentic, notwithstanding the false telegram recently sent
from Washington."

The fact is that the rebel marksmanship
caused no greater damage than inflicting a
wound upon the flag-staff of the vessel which
carried the gallant Brooklyn soldiers. As
Lieutenant Woodward was standing near the
flag-staff at the time, the splinters were scattered upon his uniform.

The next letter is dated the twenty-fifth of
May, and like the others, is from Annapolis:

All the inhabitants here concur in saying
that this is the coolest and pleasantest Spring
ever known. The weather in the main has
been beautiful, but subject, as with you, to
sudden changes. Up to the middle or end of
July, I am told, a breeze springs up at 11 A. M.
and lasts until 2 o'clock. Thus far I have
found it unfailing, and almost sufficiently
marked in its coming to enable you to set
your watch by it. In the evening it blows
back again. No matter from what quarter it

comes it is cool and refreshing. I am told there is not a stone as large as my hand to be found within twenty miles of this place, unless an imported article. The houses and outhouses are poor and dilapidated — everything about one hundred years behind this Yankee age. One acre in ten cultivated, or rather half attended to. Have seen a few good horses, owned by the wealthier residents, who are continually on horseback, and all appear to be fine riders. It seems actually cruel to deprive the cows of their milk, because they appear to need all the nourishment for themselves, and, secondly, it is of very little use to us, as owing to the abundance of garlic in all the pasturage the milk has the flavor of onion soup. Fishing plenty and good — eels, bass, and pike. Our men are constantly at it when off duty. Wild ducks have been very numerous but now have mostly left. For other hunting there is no lack of game, from all accounts, but as we are not allowed to indulge in that line I speak only from what the townsmen tell me. For song-birds we have any quantity of orioles and a good many

mocking-birds.   At daybreak the place is
fairly alive with them.   I think it was a wren
that I heard this moment in the tree by my
window.

No movement yet towards taking us from
here.   Your affectionate son,

JNO. B. W.

ANNAPOLIS, Sunday, June 2d, 1861.

We are just in the midst of preparations for
two important events, the first in order being
of unusual importance and therefore requiring
unusual care.   It is this: we have invited Colonel Smith, his wife and daughter, Mrs. Captain Thorne, and two of their lady friends of
Annapolis, to dine with us to-day.   You can
imagine our anxiety to have our quarters in
the very best possible trim.   This has at last
been secured.   The decoration of our rooms
has also been the subject of much thought,
and, thanks to Joe Leggett, (the very best fellow in the entire universe), has been done in
an exceedingly gorgeous style.   We have a
stack of arms surmounted and surrounded by
the various implements of war in our posses-

sion. The dinner is to be a superb affair, being got up by the best cook in town. An hour more and this event will have passed off. Immediately after dinner our company are ordered to embark and proceed up the river and to land detachments of ten men at convenient distances, who, under charge of non-commissioned officers, will scout the country for several miles on each side. We shall probably return to-night. I go to a point where a troop of cavalry are reported to rendezvous, who have lately, on several occasions, attacked our picket guard located about eight miles from here. We are ordered to go without muskets, relying for defense, if attacked, (a very improbable event), upon our revolvers. Next Tuesday or Wednesday one hundred of our corps, under command of Captain Thorne, are ordered to undertake an expedition, which, if successful, will give us great notoriety. I am told, (we are know-nothings as to coming events), that we go to the village, town, or city, of Princess Anne and from there strike inland to Snow Hill, where the people have gone crazy and turned Secessionists, have hoisted the rebel flag and done other rebel work. We want that flag and expect to get it. This expedition entails upon us a march of twenty miles each way, which, as it requires speed in its accomplishment, will be very apt to test the pluck and endurance of our scribblers. We do not expect any attack, but if one is made I think we shall be able to come out right side up. . . . One other matter. Our company is about 160 strong and more coming. This gives too much work for us all, and of course overcrowds very largely even our spacious quarters. It has therefore been deemed expedient to organize a new company. The initiatory steps have been taken, and the letter I given to us. The boys rebel very much against the change, as all adore Captain Thorne and refuse to be divided, unless to go under my command. I think I am not possessed of much ambition, for I look forward with great reluctance to the task in store for me, as it will be hard work where the result of my labor will not be to advance the interest or promote the comfort of Captain "Dick." I shall do my best and leave the rest to luck. Don't let this matter into all the ring, as I desire it be not known until it is an accomplished affair. It would do your old heart good could you see, as well as hear, the attachment exhibited toward me by the men, and their willingness to link their fate with mine. Almost every evening I get a comfortable place on the green and they come around me, ask questions on military affairs and explanations of movements or modes of executing various motions in the manual, until I feel as if I was a youthful reproduction of the old print where Peter Parley is shown surrounded by his friends.

ANNAPOLIS, June 9th, 1861.

..... The dinner to the ladies was in the "set out" a grand affair, but the eating was spoiled by the reception of an order that started us on the scouting expedition an hour earlier than we expected. Therefore we left the feast half finished. The scouting expedition turned out an exceedingly pleasant one to me. When our boat had proceeded about nine miles from this place Captain Thorne

6

sent me ashore with four men to see what I could see and to find out whether any forces were skulking in the neighborhood. We were landed opposite the home of Mr. Whitney, the former Attorney-General of the State, and were most hospitably received and kindly treated. Mr. Whitney, on account of his Union sentiments, was compelled to leave the city of Baltimore and take up his residence in the secluded place where we found him. His wife gave us fruit and cream, fine bouquets, and, best of all, a loaf of home-made bread. Her mother, a lady sixty-eight years of age, desired particularly that I should mention her to you and tell you that although her own son was a major in the Southern army her sympathies were all with the North, and that the happiest day she had known for years was last Sunday, when I landed and she took my hand and felt that she knew one who, being engaged in the Union cause, was dearer to her than her own son. . . . . . . To-morrow or Tuesday we leave on another expedition. Do not know more about what we are to do than I did a week ago, only that we are to go to Fortress Mon-

roe with the Winans steam gun. Returning
we will have some work to do in the southern
and eastern part of this State. I am very
glad to have an opportunity to see General
Butler again. . . . . . . Maria's letter with the
woodcut of Peter Parley has been received
and causes much amusement.

ANNAPOLIS, June 16th, 1861.

We are now in the midst of confusion attending the packing of knapsacks and the preparations necessary before starting on the expedition which I mentioned in a recent letter.
I have just come into the quarters, having
been engaged in getting the Winans steam
gun on board the propeller *Sophia*. Our mission is to take it to General Butler at Fortress
Monroe. Returning we are to stop at Princess Anne, march twenty miles to Snow Hill,
and there do something or other the details of
which have not been communicated to me.
As the soil in that portion of Maryland is, I
am told, a white sand, we look forward to a
very difficult march and one that will test to
the full the endurance of our boys; and as the

inhabitants have, in all probability, been apprised of our approach, through the foolish publicity which has been given to this expedition, we may be received in a very warm manner. Our pluck may be put to the test again. From the result attending the last two expeditions I am, however, constrained to think that we will return with " nobody hurt." I sincerely hope this may be so, but should we be drawn into a skirmish I shall endeavor to do my duty without fear of the result which may come to me. Do not get anxious about it, for I have faith that Captain Thorne will keep us all from harm. I shall telegraph to you, or cause it to be done, immediately on our return.

Presume the papers have informed you of our trip to Baltimore and safe return. The entire regiment went, and this place was left in care of a detachment of the Sixth Regiment. We had an exceedingly arduous time of it. Twenty hours without food is alone hard to bear. At ten o'clock at night we encamped in the open air. Most of us had got to sleep, when, at twelve, we were ordered to march to a train of cars, where the balance of the night was spent far more uncomfortably than if we had remained on the ground.

QUARTERS CO. G, THIRTEENTH REGIMENT,
CARROLL HILL, BALTIMORE, June 17th, 1861.

DEAR FATHER,

At the time of the last letter I wrote I thought I was to be off within five minutes for Fortress Monroe. You will see that I was in error, for here we are, in the city of Baltimore, the men just falling in for the purpose of pitching tents. We received orders on Saturday, just as our corps was formed, to march on board the propeller. The regiment was "wanted in Washington." We were rather angry at the change, but soon recovered our spirits and packed everything up in double-quick time; got on board the train about half-past three in the afternoon, yesterday. Sunday, arrived here about seven and formed camp in the open air. Being tired, most of the men were soon fast asleep. About eleven a heavy rain set in, when I started them up and took possession of an old house and outhouse where the night was spent more comfortably.

It is now threatening rain every minute, so we are all in a hurry to get our tents up. We have bid Annapolis good-bye and from appearances are about to engage in real active service, as troops are pouring in here. Of course, we are overrun with rumors as to our destination and business. Norfolk, Harper's Ferry, and Manassas Junction are the points named. The boys are all in good health, but since Thursday last we have had only two decent meals. It is now fifteen hours since we have eaten anything. We are encamped on a miserable place called Carroll Hill, but it is a hill the wrong way up, for it is a swampy piece of ground, low and wet. As we expect to be here only a day or two we shall probably not receive any harm.

CAMP BROOKLYN, MT. McCLURE,
NEAR BALTIMORE, June 19th, 1861.

. . . . . Our tents are now all up and the men pretty comfortably provided for, except that on account of the insufficient supply of tents they are very much crowded. The united action of the line officers prevented the camp's being laid out in the spot which I mentioned in my last note. We are now encamped on a hill which partially surrounds the swamp. It is not of sufficient size for the purpose, but it is much better than the other place. The soil is very bad, brick clay, and our camp is surrounded by the brick-kilns. Of course the grass grows very poorly, and what little there was has been worn off, so that we are terribly dirty. The mud sticks to our feet, tracks into our tents, and holds fast as flour to our clothes. The utmost disgust is displayed by our nice young men when they ruefully survey their uniforms. There is but one tree within our camp lines and I am now writing beneath its shade, where I am comparatively comfortable. In camp the light of this white clay and the tents, in the sun in the middle of the day, is almost unbearable. Still, in spite of these discomforts all our men prefer being here to their late quarters in Annapolis. It seems more like what we came for. I have traveled some in Baltimore and have experienced no trouble, save that when asking information in regard to streets and places saucy

and provoking answers are frequently returned. We, however, take no notice of them.
There is no doubt that two-thirds of the inhabitants are Secessionists and make no bones
of saying so. The police are disloyal to a man.
It is therefore impossible to get a decent reply
from them. I asked one yesterday where Baltimore Street was, knowing at the time it was
only a block off. His answer was "Just fifty-
nine blocks up street." . . . . . A great number
of troops passed through here yesterday and
to-day. Some big movement is on foot. Don't
know whether we are to be counted in or sent
home. Rumors each way are very plenty.
General Banks reviewed us yesterday. My
health is good once more.

COLEMAN'S EUTAW HOUSE,
BALTIMORE, Sunday, June 23d, 1861.

On the 23d of June, 1854, I was elected a
member of the Brooklyn City Guard. That
was seven years ago to-day. I am therefore
out of my time, and I feel as I imagine an ap-
prentice feels when his time is out. If I had
more money I would have a blow out, but as

Uncle Sam does n't pony up I must wait until supplied with the sinews of a spree. . . .

COLEMAN'S EUTAW HOUSE,
BALTIMORE, June 30th, 1861.

This is my first appearance outside of camp since I last wrote at this table, with the exception of Thursday last, when our regiment made a parade through some of the principal streets of the city. In some spots we were well received; in others cheers for Jeff Davis were heard, and two heroic young ladies waved Secession flags at us. They were not molested. Our orders are now very strict. No one is allowed outside the camp. To-day I am, therefore, for the first time, away without permission; but as we have no convenience for bathing at or near the camp, and as I felt that it was absolutely necessary to have a clean wash and shave once a week, I have taken the risk.

QUARTERS CO. G, THIRTEENTH REGIMENT,
BALTIMORE CITY PRISON, July 3d, 1861.

DEAR FATHER,

You will think this a pretty place for a son of yours to be stationed, especially as it wants

7

only four hours of the glorious Fourth of
July. But here I am, and here the gallant
Company G are, and, I presume, will remain
for a day or two longer. We are inside the
walls and under lock and key, but, thank fortune, the key is in our hands. Our duty is to
take care of the place and the ward, (the 8th),
in which it is situated. . . . The Secesh are
still far more plucky than the Unionists, and
the young women are particularly impudent
in the display of embroidered rebel flags on
their handkerchiefs and basques. We return
their unladylike salutations in our usual gallant manner. Stutzer very kindly, (and I
fully appreciate it), sent me a letter of introduction and credit to a business firm here,
friends of his. I delivered it and was sorry to
learn that on account of their Southern views
it would be impossible for them to recognize
me, further than to pay my drafts, whilst I
wore the uniform of a Northern regiment.
The member of the firm said that if I would
come to him in citizen's apparel they would
gladly extend any and every attention in their
power; but as I think it not consistent with

my duty to purchase any personal comfort at the cost of my identity as a Northern soldier I withdrew the letter, giving the gentleman a hint, in the politest manner in the world, that I wished neither money nor favor from an enemy of my government and my country. I returned the letter to Mr. Stutzer with explanations and hope he will endorse my action in the matter.

QUARTERS G Co., THIRTEENTH REGIMENT,
BALTIMORE CITY PRISON, July 7th, 1861.

You will observe that we are still behind bolts and bars, but as we are comfortable we do not object. Yesterday a negro sentenced for larceny was sold as a slave for one year, to the highest bidder. I bought him for ten dollars. I am therefore a slave owner, and have got my property now as a servant, but I intend to let him go to-morrow. He is a very good fellow. Has taken a desperate fancy to me and declares he won't leave "his marster"; but, as I bought him for the sake of his mother, who has washed for me since my arrival in Baltimore, and not for my own benefit, I shall present him to her. In this State a free negro is sold as a slave for the length of time for which a white man is imprisoned. The State is therefore saved expense and the negro benefited. The boys poke a good deal of fun at me and my purchase; but I don't mind it, as I think I have spent ten dollars as wisely as I ever did any similar amount. [Only a few days before his death General Woodward met this man near the Down Town Club in New York.]

CAMP BROOKLYN, BALTIMORE, July 20th, 1861.

Owing to the absence of the Adjutant I have been detailed to fill the position. I have therefore double duty to perform and only the same time to do it in. I am now writing at the table occupied by the court martial, who are now in session, and my attention is momentarily called away as the men make their various excuses for being absent from parade.

We expect to be in Brooklyn next Wednesday or Thursday. It seems hardly possible that we can be so near our time of return, and as it gets nearer and nearer I feel less desire to have it come. We are now so comfortably located that it appears too bad to break up the associations of camp and return to civilized life. I hardly think you can keep me home unless you rig up a tent on the grass plot and find some one to bang at a drum pretty early in the morning.

The regiment returned to New York on the thirtieth of July, when the members were at once mustered out. Lieutenant Woodward resumed the habits of commercial life but gave strict attention to his regimental duties, feeling certain that he would be called on for service again.

Before leaving this eventful period in the life of the young soldier it may be well to quote some expressions in the letter of a private of his company, written to his uncle in Brooklyn, from the headquarters of the regiment at Annapolis, on the twenty-sixth of May:

..... How proud we all are of John. Every one loves him: he is the backbone of good order and is very careful in looking after our comfort. We would follow him anywhere; and his courage and bravery are equal to any emergency.

III

SERVICE WITH THE UNION ARMY IN 1862

ON the twelfth of November Lieutenant Woodward was elected Captain of Company E, Thirteenth Regiment. His parting with his old company was quite affecting, and he would not have accepted the promotion if he had not been fully persuaded that it opened for him a larger field of usefulness and presented him an imperative call of duty. On the twenty-fifth of January, 1862, he was elected Lieutenant-Colonel of the regiment. A few months later the rebel army of Virginia made a sudden advance northward. The army of the Potomac under General McClellan was on the Peninsula, endeavoring to reach Richmond. As a counter movement Stonewall Jackson advanced up the Shenandoah Valley and struck Banks' army, which retreated to Harper's Ferry in disorder.

Washington was again in danger and President Lincoln appealed for a second time to the Northern States. As in the previous year the response of New York was prompt and effective. Within nine days after the call twelve regiments of National Guardsmen completely armed and equipped, averaging seven hundred men each, were hurried to the front. The Thirteenth Regiment was among those called out. The order for its departure was issued on May twenty-sixth, 1862, and on the thirtieth it marched, seven hundred and sixty-two strong. Before the departure the leather merchants in "The Swamp" presented Lieutenant-Colonel Woodward with a horse. As the regiment went through the streets of Brooklyn it was escorted by a large committee of citizens, the buildings were profusely decorated, the firemen and other associations were drawn up on either side of the streets, and the entire community turned out to wish the men Godspeed.

The regiment was at first ordered to Fort McHenry, near Baltimore, where it remained until June fifth, when it was sent to Fortress Monroe. Upon Colonel Woodward's reporting to Major-General Dix he received orders for the Thirteenth to proceed to Norfolk, which had just been evacuated by the Confederates. Passing through Norfolk, the regiment marched to Suffolk, where it was mustered in for a second term of three months. During this period the men patrolled and protected the debatable land lying between the Weldon Railroad and the city of Norfolk, which was menaced by rebel troops. The force with which it was associated was small, and it was constantly employed in marching, scouting, and similar services. It was engaged in several skirmishes, but no serious attack was made during its enlistment.

The following letters from Lieutenant-Colonel Woodward describe the incidents of his service. His father was still living, and it was to him that most of the letters were addressed.

CAMP NEAR FORT MCHENRY,
BALTIMORE, June 1st, 1862.

DEAR FATHER,

We arrived at this locality at 3 o'clock yesterday afternoon after a most tedious trip of twenty-two hours. The train was exceedingly large and heavy, and slow in its movements; but so very brief in the stops at the various towns that the men were afforded no opportunity for obtaining anything to eat. As the last meal I ate was Friday morning's breakfast I was terribly used up Saturday evening at supper time; in fact, so much so, and I was suffering so from neuralgia in my head, that the Surgeon took military possession of me and sent me into town and to the Eutaw House as "unfit for service." I never was in greater suffering in my life than from noon until midnight yesterday, when I got to sleep. I woke up this morning feeling almost myself again. Shortly after we arrived on the campingground, (which is situated just outside the fort, on very low, damp ground, almost a swamp), a most terrific thunderstorm came up, before the men had any opportunity to pitch a tent. Our new uniforms were in a few moments wet through. We were fortunate in finding a large building in the neighborhood vacant. It was soon filled with the Thirteenth and for the balance of the night they received no more wetting from the rain,

8

which continued to fall until morning. It is
now raining heavily, but the tents are all up
and we can keep dry if not comfortable. To-
day I got on the ground at nine o'clock, and,
although feeling very slim, have been hard at
work and am very much used up again, but
am not sick. The horse Tanner behaved ad-
mirably during the trip. He was placed in a
box-car and took things as coolly as if he was
accustomed to railroad life. When we arrived
at the camp ground I found a deserted stable,
put him in it, had him watered and fed, and I
believe he passed the night comfortably. He
is very much admired by all. . . . Crowds of
the citizens who made acquaintances in the
regiment when we were last here have been
up to renew them, and they will strongly urge
upon General Wool, (who, we are told, is to
relieve General Dix here), to retain us in this
department.

HEADQUARTERS THIRTEENTH REGIMENT N. Y. S. M.,
     CAMP CRESCENT, BALTIMORE, June 5th, 1862.
                         Midnight.

I have just been awoke from a sound sleep.
Find an order from headquarters directing the

preparation of the regiment for departure to Fortress Monroe. As the Colonel is ill I have my hands full and cannot write more. The orders are to be ready to start at 12 M. to-morrow. The presence of so many troops there will render it a very uncomfortable trip.

ON BOARD U. S. TRANSPORT BALLOON,
HAMPTON ROADS, VA., June 7th, 1862.

I am here in command of four companies, A, C, F, and G, in this little North River steamer. The balance of the regiment is behind us some ten or twelve hours, on board the steamer *Star*. We left Baltimore at seven o'clock in the evening and arrived off Fortress Monroe at ten o'clock this morning. I went ahead and reported to General Dix, who ordered me to proceed immediately to Suffolk. I am to go on and establish a post there before the arrival of the balance of the regiment. Whilst I write we are on the passage from the Fortress to Norfolk, where we shall arrive in an hour and immediately take the cars for Suffolk. The Third and Fourth New York Volunteers and the Thirteenth and Twenty-fifth regiments of militia are to be stationed there. Although all were in Baltimore together I have the honor of having first reported at the Fortress, and I intend to be the first on the ground.

Landing at Fortress Monroe I was compelled to pass through a hospital ship. In the very first cot I saw John Echalaz, who was in Saturday's fight with the First Regiment Chasseurs and lost his leg. He looks very ill. He was on the *State of Maine* and I am told will be taken to New Haven.

Getting away down here in Secessia is rather more than we bargained for, but we must make the best of it. Most of the men are pleased, but some of the officers prefer going home or to Washington. The arms furnished are not good for anything, and as it has rained ever since we have been here the drill is very deficient.

ON BOARD TRANSPORT BALLOON,
NORFOLK, VA., June 8th, 1862.

Immediately the boat touched the dock the Quartermaster and I jumped ashore and made

our way to the custom house, which is used
by General Viele as his headquarters. I found
him and reported for orders, which were given
me to proceed at once to Suffolk. On reach-
ing the boat again I was surprised and an-
noyed to find that the Ordnance Sergeant had
neglected to provide me with a single round of
cartridges. I immediately notified the General of the fact, which caused him to grumble.
He asked me to go on without it, which I
promised to do, but he afterwards changed
his mind and we are now awaiting the balance of the regiment, which will be here in
a few hours, when we shall probably go ahead.
What remains of the navy yard is in sight,
and Portsmouth, opposite, looks like a peaceful country place. In fact, there is nothing
alarming to be seen in any direction. My orders are so strict to keep all my men on board
that I have not had the courage to go ashore
and enjoy a privilege denied them. I can
therefore speak only of what was to be seen
in the few squares between the dock and the
custom house. All the stores appear to be
closed, except a few small retail concerns, and

the place looks as deserted as can be ima-
gined. The Union feeling exists only in homeopathic cases and they are as yet afraid to
come out squarely and say what they mean.
Take a walk on Front or Water Street, New
York, on a Sunday, and you have an exact
idea of what Norfolk appears to be. The few
women who remain pull their dresses aside
and avoid a uniform as they would a pot
of tar. Our orders are extremely rigorous
against entering houses uninvited, or taking
any article, however small, without payment.
Either will be punished by the arrest of the
Captain of the company of which the offender
is a member and the confinement of the man at
the Rip-Raps. On our passage up the Elizabeth River we found forces busily engaged in
blowing the enemy's earthworks to pieces.
The reports are frequent and very heavy.
. . . It is hard work to get change here without taking a lot of shinplasters, and a good
many dollars are now in the mail on the way
home as curiosities. I have threatened to arrest any one who sends any more, as it is aid-
ing and abetting the rebellion. . . . Our offi-

cers' mess costs like blazes in this place, as
you will see by the bill for our breakfast to-
day. Ham fifteen cents per pound, eggs
twenty-five cents per pound, butter thirty-
seven and a half cents per pound, cheese eighteen cents per pound, radishes five cents per
bunch, lemons one shilling each, ice one dollar
per hundredweight. Milk we cannot get.

HEADQUARTERS THIRTEENTH REGIMENT N. G. N. Y.,
    CAMP CROOKE, SUFFOLK, VA., June 10th, 1862.

I send enclosed a sketch of the positions of
the pickets as I found them posted. It will
show you what a beautiful muss the place is
in. Three or four avenues of approach which
are not laid down are entirely unguarded.
The sketch and report have scared General
Max Webber, and he has just left the camp
with the new officer of the day, Major Abel
Smith, Jr., for the purpose of rearranging and
posting anew the outposts and picket stations.
Any child would have done better than Colonel ——, who has been in command. . . . . .
Suffolk is the meanest God-forsaken place
you ever saw — houses deserted, stores shut

up, darkies, hounds, and poor white trash being the only objects seen. Those having anything to sell refuse entirely, or, perhaps, will
consent to let you have a little if you will pay
in Confederate shinplasters or silver; and as I
have not either I find hard work to get the
necessities of life. The country around is extremely level and low. It is, in fact, the wind-
ing up of the Dismal Swamp. Under our tent
floor we have a well with plenty of milk-col-
ored water which tastes very good and is
reached by digging about eighteen inches.
During the heavy rains, which have lasted now
two days, all the water appears to lie on top of
the ground, but it disappears mysteriously the
moment the sun shines. Two hours ago the
mud was three inches deep, now it is almost
dusty. General Webber told me this morning
that he had news of the capture of Memphis
and the total clearance of the Mississippi
River of rebel gunboats. I have just written
an order to be read to the men at evening parade announcing the fact. Glory enough for
one day. This news will have an inspiring
effect here.

HEADQUARTERS THIRTEENTH REGIMENT N. G. N. Y.,
CAMP CROOKE, SUFFOLK, VA., Sunday, June 15th, 1862.

. . . . . Since the day when I was on duty as field officer we have been exempt from rain, but have been almost burned up with the heat, which is intense during the day notwithstanding a constant westerly breeze.

The two great discomforts of our camp life are the impossibility of securing supplies for our mess, and, second, the insect world, wood-ticks, flies, and mosquitos. The inhabitants of Suffolk will not sell anything for a Union officer to eat. Our men are treated precisely the same as if they were in Baltimore or New York, the Quartermaster's stores being here in full supply. We have been obliged to sponge on the men. Yesterday six of us made a breakfast from two small spring chickens and hardtack, nothing for dinner, bread and molasses for supper. This morning a red herring apiece, coffee, and hardtack; for dinner mush and molasses. What supper time will bring I cannot say; but as our sutler has just arrived and is carting his stores upon the ground I have hopes of filling up on something or

9

other. The insect world we fight during the
day with both hands and a handkerchief. At
night I fix them by wearing an arrangement
some Yankee has invented. It is made of mos-
quito netting in the shape of a feed-bag kept
distended by whalebone rings. When you lie
down the rings keep the netting three or four
inches from your face. I found I could not do
without one of these contrivances. The wood-
ticks, however, are not to be baffled. We
have to pick them out on the point of a knife
whenever we find them upon us. The wounds
are far more uncomfortable than the lumps
caused by the pigeon-sized mosquitos which
the Dismal Swamp supplies us.

Our Chaplain proves a very good fellow;
smokes a cigar but prefers a pipe, is fond of
a joke, tells a good story, knows how to laugh,
does n't grumble or get in the way, attends to
the spiritual welfare of the men, and does n't
annoy us with advice upon temporal affairs.
He has found a contraband and is indus-
triously laboring to improve and educate him.
Has succeeded in driving ten or twelve letters
of the alphabet into his head but cannot teach

him to be frugal and to eat the crusts of the slices of bread he has for dinner. He has concluded that to own thirty or forty slaves must be a terrible task. I am sure the darky is disgusted with the Chaplain, and I rather suspect the feeling is becoming mutual. . . . . . I very much fear the work which to-morrow is to give us, as the regiment is then to be sworn into service. Had this formality been gone through at Brooklyn or at Baltimore all would have been well; but now some of the officers, whose hearts ought to have been put in chickens' breasts, intend to back down and refuse to swear in, giving as a reason that they enlisted and left home to do garrison duty and not to fight, to play soldier at Washington or Baltimore but not to do soldier's work and share a soldier's danger at Suffolk or anywhere else in any place where an enemy could by any possibility be scared up. Well, we will let them go their own way, as Captain Russell did the deacons, hoping Brooklyn, like this camp, may prove too warm for their comfort. Besides these, the Surgeon refuses to accept some fifty or sixty who had enlisted, on account of their

having permanent disabilities. These have to
go, willingly or not. Trouble will arise in ex-
pelling them from the camp and forcing them
to get on the train. The slinks we will have
trouble with, as we intend to send them away
in disgrace; but when we do get rid of them
we shall have very healthy and brave men —
far better material than any other regiment in
the service — and probably six hundred and
fifty of them. . . . . . General Mansfield has
arrived and taken command. He is one of the
nicest old gentlemen I have met in military
life. He is exceedingly good to us and very
approachable. General Webber, in whose brigade we are, is said to be a good and brave
officer. His Assistant-Adjutant-General, Captain ———, got his fingers burned by me the
other day when he thought a militia Lieutenant-Colonel could be bossed around by a three-
year volunteer Captain. Found out his mis-
take and is now decently civil. We three-
months men are considered poor truck and
know-nothings, but so far we have beaten the
three-year men regularly in every change of
location and are always first at brigade guard-

mounting. We were smart enough to get our men transferred here on the railroad. They marched. They don't like it; but we have got them on the hip, and if we ever get into a scrimmage I do hope we shall finish up the only remaining matter and outfight them.

After an examination of the country and the maps I am convinced that there will be no attempt made by the rebels to repossess this place. When they evacuated Norfolk they burned and destroyed the navy yard; along the railroad, even thirty miles further out than where we are, they have destroyed the bridges; they have removed a couple of dams and overflowed a piece of ground, which renders our defense in case of an attack from that quarter perfect; they have removed their records to Danville, N. C.; Burnside has made arrangements to march to Weldon, which is on the railroad connected with us; and I cannot see any advantage that would be gained for them by repossessing Suffolk. I think they have abandoned it forever. We keep our pickets and grand guard formed and instruct them to be very particular, as the enemy are

only five or ten miles away. This keeps the
men active. I believe there is no force, except guerrillas, or " gorillas " as we call them,
within thirty miles. We have plenty of false
alarms and rumors. At three o'clock this
morning the officer of the guard woke me up
and got me out of the tent in a terrible hurry
to see some signals which were being made by
the enemy. It proved to be the morning star
just rising over the woods, and owing to a
haze or smoke it looked as the moon frequently does when rising, exceedingly large
and red. The man was positive that it was a
fire balloon and meant something of advantage
to the enemy. The night before the officer of
the picket guard hauled me two miles away to
the outpost, at two o'clock in the morning, as
he saw parties in a house make signals with
red and white lights. I got there, woke up
the family, and found that the sickness of a
little child had caused the father to go down
stairs three times, making the light show in
the windows of the two stories, some of which
had a sort of tan-colored shade. . . . . . We
drill one hour before breakfast, by squad, one

hour and a half after, by company, and two hours in the evening, by battalion.

The really active service of the regiment, and the reliance which General Mansfield placed in its efficiency, are evidenced by a hastily written autograph note of that General's which has been preserved among General Woodward's papers, and is as follows:

LIEUTENANT-COLONEL WOODWARD, Officer Day:

Please investigate that matter without delay. I have a mounted rifle company on the South Quay Road, and this may be a party mounted to cut them off.

MANSFIELD, B. G., U. S. A.

The next letter from Lieutenant-Colonel Woodward is from Camp Crooke, Suffolk, where the regiment was still located, and is dated

11:15 P. M., June 19th, 1862.

DEAR FATHER,

I have this moment come into my tent from a march which was taken to ascertain the cause of an alarm which rooted all out about

an hour ago. The camp was as quiet as if
Nature was alone and soldiers unheard of.
Most of us had turned in, but few were asleep.
Suddenly we heard a shot fired from the pickets we have stationed about a quarter of a
mile out on the road which runs past our
camp; then another, and another, until some
twenty had been fired. The third shot got us
all up. The drums were rolled, the men rapidly took their places in their companies, and
our regimental line was formed. All this almost before you could say Jack Robinson.
No confusion or scurry, but the calm, cool
swiftness which betokens men who appreciate
what is required of them. Immediately after
the line was formed bayonets were fixed,
pieces were loaded, and we stood ready for
whatever might turn up. The firing had
ceased and all was quiet; still, it was our
duty to find out the cause of the alarm, so I
took Company G, (my old pets), and marched
them to the picket station, where I found that
one of the guard had accidentally, (as he first
stated, or else being alarmed at something, he
did not know what), fired his piece. Each of

the other posts also fired his piece for the purpose of passing the alarm in. This was all. No enemy, no danger, and our pains for nothing. Yet I do not regret it, for it has taught me that we have a very reliable, good set of men. Better order or a better sudden formation could not be had. As the man who fired his piece prevaricated I arrested him and have brought him into camp and have got him under guard. Generals Mansfield and Webber were soon upon the ground and passed a well-deserved compliment to our boys. This seems a small matter to write about, but as it is the first incident of the sort in the campaign I think it worth relating. You must remember that we are in the very heart of the secession country, that a guerrilla band is not many miles away, and the cry of wolf must not be carelessly heard. . . . To-day we had our first battalion drill, Generals Mansfield and Webber being present. The regiment really did well. General Mansfield requested us to go through several movements. He expressed much surprise at the very correct performance of them, and we

10

now stand well on the General's books. We
beat all the regiments here in promptness and
correctness of our official business. The white
feather men left for home to-day. Give them
a scorching reception.

The next letter from Camp Crooke is dated
the eighteenth of June, and is addressed to a
sister.

DEAR MARIA,

. . . . . I am very glad that the swearing in
is over and that so few men have left us. . . .
. . It was my turn yesterday at inspecting the
pickets, or being field officer of the day, so I
feel pretty nearly used up, having been the
round three times, making a ride of nearly
fifty miles. I used two horses, first Tanner
and then a borrowed one. The thermometer
stood at about ninety and the sun was shining
furiously. I cannot say the ride was very
agreeable. The place where we are encamped
has been occupied for many months by three
or four rebel regiments, and the log huts
where they wintered partly remain, notwithstanding the conflagration that they caused

when the place was evacuated some three weeks ago. The huts must have been very comfortable and are quite picturesque, being very neatly made. Some of them have windows and very nice window-shades. The men are continually rooting and scraping among the rubbish for trophies. One succeeded in finding a gold watch, another a pistol. These instances of luck, however, are rare, the principal articles found being buttons.

June 23d, 1862.

I have not yet allowed two days to pass without writing to someone at home. . . . . . Tanner is improving as a saddle-horse. Last night he broke loose in his stable, knocked the door down, and left for Dixie. He was caught by the outside pickets, after being nearly shot, as he refused to halt when challenged. I did not miss him until seven o'clock, and was, of course, in much tribulation until the picket, who recognized him, brought him into camp. . . . . . I have eaten onions in as liberal a manner as my exchequer will permit. Six cents each comes too high, except for luxuries. Vegetables of all sorts are always in short sup-

ply here. The people are too lazy to raise
them, and don't appear to care much for them.
My health has been capital since coming upon
this ground. I think it is owing much to the
coolness of the evenings, so that I am enabled
to sleep soundly. I cannot remember when I
have slept so well from tattoo to reveille every
night. I prefer the mosquitos to pennyroyal,
so I sleep through their attacks at night and
they never raise itching spots on my flesh.
To-day I have been on duty again as field officer of the day and I have had quite an uncomfortable time. The morning opened very hot.
Horse and self perspired remarkably freely.
At noon the clouds began to gather, and at
1 P. M. I reached my tent, (after a rapid ride
through a piece of woods, where I had to follow a footpath, the branches of the trees
scratching me badly), just in time to escape
a terrible drenching. This afternoon it was
very pleasant and I enjoyed my rounds very
much.

July 25th, 1862.

Still here and all quiet along the line of the
Nansemond. . . . . . I received an order yes-

terday detailing the Colonel and myself as members of a court martial to try the Lieutenant-Colonel and Major of the Fourth New York Volunteers. . . . . . My health remains first rate, but I am very tired, as, owing to the absence of two, and the sickness of two other, field officers, I have been on duty forty-eight out of the last seventy-two hours.

July 5th, 1862.

. . . . . . Last year, you will remember, I spent the glorious Fourth in the city jail of Baltimore. Yesterday I sat from nine to three on my three-legged stool in the court room. The scene is shifted but the connection remains. The second act was played before the first. I did not hear a solitary firecracker. I shall forget what the Fourth of July is if another year finds me suppressing the rebellion. . . . . . . We are all very anxious for news from the Peninsula. We hear rumors daily, but our newspapers, the only means of information, are two days old when they reach us, and that is a long time in this age of steam and telegraph. I saw General Webber this

morning and asked if the news was better.
"Vell, I shall hope to tell you somedings by
und by. Vat I tell you now is not much
happy." The troops prefer Webber to Mansfield, as the former is a very fine-looking man
and is much more with us. They judge by
Mansfield's white head and beard that he is
too old-fogy. For my part I like the "old un"
best. I am on good terms with him and we
often teach each other something about military matters.

July 6th, 1862.

To-day is Sunday, and although it is said,
and with some truth, that a soldier does not
know one day from another, yet I am sure no
one could look into this camp without being
impressed with the extra quiet. The clean
boots and shirts and neatly brushed clothes,
the very demeanor of the men, prove that all
do know, and endeavor to show by the pro-
priety of their conduct that they honor, the
day. It is one of the best evidences of the
fine class of men we have, and that the home
influence still surrounds them.

July 8th, 1862.

Whew! We have got it now. Imagine the hottest day you ever saw and then fry it and you will approximate the heat we endured yesterday and are enduring to-day. Yesterday it marked in a cool place 105°, and no breeze. At half-past six we commenced battalion drill, which had been postponed from four o'clock. In ten minutes five men had fainted and been carried off, so I sent the regiment all to their quarters. We shall not try it again until the weather moderates. I shall, however, take advantage of the fine moonlight now in season. . . . Our regiment is practised daily now at target shooting. I wanted to try Tanner under fire. Find he takes it as quietly as slapping your hands. To-day I took him out when the artillery was at work firing blank cartridges; rode him within ten feet of a gun when it was being fired; after three discharges he took it calmly; let the reins fall over his neck and the only notice he took was to prick up his ears; did not move his feet. So, if we do get in action I hardly think it will be necessary to pay any

attention to him. I practise him daily in
jumping ditches, and will shortly try fences.
Yesterday I jumped a ditch eight feet wide,
from a halt, which is doing pretty well. He
does not like that kind of work but spurs are
good coaxers.

July 16th, 1862.

. . . Monday the 14th I was on duty as
field officer of the day. Every time I am
mounted on a "sissing" hot day I think I
would suffer less with the heat if I were on
foot. When I am on foot I prefer to be
mounted. I have not made up my mind
which is the cooler mode of locomotion. I
made the rounds five times and was in the
saddle all night. Yesterday I was not worth
a rap, the exertion having used me all up.
My tent, being peculiarly pitched, is regarded
as a cool place, so my friends, who are numerous, desire to share its shade. I was also
called upon to entertain four officers from the
Army of the Potomac. That night I slept
forty knots an hour and this morning awoke
feeling like a lark. I expected a cool, comfortable day would follow such a storm as we

had last night, but instead of cooling it appears to have heightened the temperature. Troubles never come singly and to-day we were ordered to the first of our brigade drills. We left the camp at four o'clock, the field officers being mounted. The brigade drill ground is a most beautiful one, being an oblong of some eight hundred by twelve hundred paces, formerly cultivated as a corn-field. We chose to go across country and it was quite amusing to see the regiment moving in regular order over ditches, fences, &c. I jumped the obstacles and am getting to be an expert at the business. We arrived first upon the ground but were soon followed by the balance of the brigade. The line was formed and the drill commenced. The heat was intense and the men of the Third, Fourth, and Twenty-fifth regiments fell like sheep, and the drum corps were kept busy carrying them off. Our boys stood it wonderfully and we did not lose more than a dozen. The Third must have had eighty to a hundred lying in the shade of the fence. Colonel Bryan of the Twenty-fifth and Lieutenant-Colonel Mc-

11

Gregor of the Third both came tumbling from their horses, and twice I was so much overcome as to be unable to see Tanner's ears, but my will was too strong for the flesh and I got through, not without considerable suffering. Major Boyd being too sick to go to the drill I had double duty and my poor horse looked as if he had been ducked in the river.

General Max Webber is a splendid officer and handled the brigade beautifully, the only drawback being that his orders are occasionally not quite clear, owing to his peculiar pronunciation of the words. He understands English perfectly. He is like Stutzer, never gets the cart before the horse. He kept us at it until six o'clock, when, becoming overpowered by the heat himself, we were dismissed. . . . I have applications daily for passes by men who want to get specimens of bugs and such things for me. Yesterday a very bright looking boy came and I gave him a pass. He returned in a couple of hours with a basket which he had ingeniously made by cutting the bark of a tree clear around and putting in a bottom. He then filled it with blackberries, which he handed to me, saying, "Colonel, them's better than derned nasty bugs and lizards." I agree exactly with him, and that youth can have a pass as long as the berries last.

July 19th, 1862.

. . . . . In a stroll through the adjacent woods, fields, and swamps I found to-day two flowers, in great abundance, and the long reed or cane which is used for fishing-poles. I enclose a flower, and regret my envelope will not hold a fine pole which I cut. It must be twenty feet long.

July 22d, 1862.

Rumors are still flying around and the "old grannies" are trembling, and their "lumbago" is suddenly worse, on account of a statement that a cavalry force of three hundred which went out yesterday on a reconnoissance have sent in for reinforcements and that they have discovered a force of five thousand rebels on the Blackwater, a river twenty miles distant. As nothing is known of the matter at headquarters perhaps we may live through the night safely. . . . . . Our sick men still hang

on without any material change. The health
of the camp remains excellent. The First
Delaware has ninety-six men in hospital.
They have buried four. We have only six
sick. I cannot account for this great discrep-
ancy unless the explanation is found in an ap-
ple orchard which is along side of their camp.

July 28th, 1862.

. . . . . . Last night the Colonel and I took
a ride. I beat him all to thunder. Tanner
has not stumbled for a long time now and I
am in hopes he has forgotten how. Saturday
I was riding in company with Major Abel
Smith, Jr., who rides a magnificent Ethan
Allen stallion, Monarque. Of course we had
a trial of speed, and if you could have seen
us tear down the ravine, over stumps, stones,
and briers, you, like myself, would have had
serious doubts of the safety of your first son's
neck and his horse's knees. At a recent brigade drill we were exercised in volley and file
firing, using ball cartridges. There is nothing
in the world which excites horses so much as
the latter, and it was truly gay. Every horse

on the field was up and doing, and Tanner being very powerful, I, of course, had my hands full. Colonel McGregor's horse took him clear off the field. Mine I managed to keep within a hundred yards of the regiment, but it took both hands, spurs, and curb to do it. We had a good deal of fun. The volley firing they did not object to so much.

August 1st, 1862.

...... The rumors in the papers of "probable attack" on this place are, I think, without foundation. Contrabands report a large force at Petersburg and some few troops nearer this way. No force exists this side of the Blackwater, and there are only some nine hundred there. Guerrillas are seen almost daily and every now and then one is caught and brought in. They constitute a sort of independent picket and convey from house to house tidings of any unusual movement here. They also stop rebel deserters and contrabands from coming in. Their actions are a disgrace to humanity. A party of our cavalry while out scouting stopped recently at the farm of an old gentleman and he allowed them to water their horses at his well and gave the officers and men a good lunch. For this he was caught and killed by the Nansemond cavalry. The brutes cut off his ears and both hands as trophies and nailed them to the gate-posts. . . . . . I always get father's birthday wrong; and on that day we made a toast to him at the midnight relief.

We have several very sick and the weather is too warm for them. Dodge, the hospital steward, died, and was buried night before last. We put him in the same ground used by the Secession regiments. It was the most impressive funeral I ever attended. The grove consists of large pine-trees, very dense. The regiment was formed in hollow square, four ranks around the grave. Everything was still as death, except the Dead March, and the Chaplain was very solemn in his remarks. Captain Briggs goes home to-day on sick leave. I fear he will never come back. Five or six men are to be discharged to-morrow for disability. We are, however, better off than any other regiment here, as we pay the strict-est attention to the cleanliness of the tents and their ventilation. To-morrow if the weather is fair every tent on the field will be down, the floors taken out, rubbish removed, and the tents again put up.

I am the field officer of the day again. A brigade drill ordered for this afternoon. Major Boyd too sick to assist me. Captain Thorne has on the last two occasions taken Boyd's place. If he were not here I don't know how I could get along.

August 3d, 1862.

It is now half-past eleven, but as I am to have the regiment under arms at half-past two in the morning I think I will make a night of it. I feel a little nervous and have tried in vain to get to sleep. The General has ordered me not to tell a single soul in the regiment that they are to come out at that hour; and as he will see for himself how prompt we can be in an emergency I want the men to move on a little more than double quick.

(August 4th.) The line was formed in

seven minutes and the square in four more. No drums beaten nor any noise made.

There are some apprehensions that this place is to be attacked very shortly, and "Old Womansfield," as our men call him, has been digging rifle-pits, building *chevaux-de-frise*, erecting stockades and many other military devices to give the fellows fits if they should come, which to my mind is very far from probable. The old General is very pious, *for a general*, and says tut! tut! when any one swears in his hearing. Talking to me to-day he said, "Now, I suppose if three hundred or four hundred cavalry should come in they would cut you and the Twenty-fifth all to pieces." You can guess my reply, for he said, "Tut! tut!" He can suppose as much as he pleases, but I'll be d—arned if they would.

August 14th, 1862.

. . . You will have heard, probably, of the death of Corporal Holt of E Company. They call it a melancholy accident. I call it gross carelessness. He was a member of picket guard No. 2, posted on the railroad. Their

guard had been relieved and were coming
into camp, marching down the track. Grand
guard No. 1 of the Fourth New York Volunteers had also been relieved and were coming
towards our camp on the mill bridge road.
When nearly up to the camp the officer of the
grand guard halted his men, faced them toward the railroad track, and they discharged
their pieces by volley. The bullets flew directly into our picket. Poor Guy was the
only one struck. The escape of the others is
simply miraculous. . . . As usual in such
cases the victim was one of the very best soldiers in the regiment and I presume more
generally known throughout than any other.
He is the son of old Mr. Holt, ("Father
Holt"), whom I think you have seen playing
baseball.

August 18th, 1862.

. . . You will, perhaps, have heard of the
anticipated attack on this town last Friday,
and as the matter may be magnified in some
accounts I think it proper that you should
know it was a very small affair. On that day
I was field officer, and at twelve o'clock, noon,

12

the sergeant of cavalry picket No. 2 rode hastily to my quarters and said that information had been received through contrabands coming in that a large force of cavalry and infantry were coming upon us. It being my duty to attend to such matters I immediately mounted and rode out to the picket, found other contrabands coming in, all of whom told the same story, with the exception that it was all cavalry. By and by the cavalry dwindled down from one thousand to four hundred, which latter number is about correct. I notified Generals Mansfield and Webber and in company with the latter made a reconnoissance some distance beyond the pickets. The conclusion that we arrived at was that the Nansemond cavalry had come from where they are encamped, (the Blackwater), for the purpose of endeavoring to cut off two of our cavalry companies who had been sent out scouting the evening previous. Fortunately the rebels were unsuccessful in their endeavor. General Mansfield sent all the cavalry in the place after them, but they heard of it and skedaddled. To-day we have another rumor of intended attack, but I have no idea that there is any foundation for it.

August 24th, 1862.

Another alarm was caused last Tuesday by the reappearance of the Nansemond cavalry, who came near our picket lines but made no other demonstration. I was again officer of the day and tried hard to overtake and corner them, but without success. As every alarm has occurred on a day that I have been field officer they have got the joke fastened on me. My turn comes again on Tuesday next and I look for another fruitless tear around the country.

In another letter, written about the time of the preceding, Lieutenant-Colonel Woodward said:

Our men are now beginning to feel some confidence in themselves, and, I hope, in their officers. I never worked harder to win the good opinion of men. I think I have in a measure succeeded, but, being a disciplinarian, I have no doubt many have got their backs up a little. Generals Webber and Mansfield were both at the drill last evening. I was in command. Mansfield was desirous of testing me to see if I knew my business, and ordered me to perform certain inversion movements, (inversion means to do a movement, as you would say, the other side up), which are exceedingly intricate; but being aware of the General's fondness for those movements I have recently made myself familiar with them. We did them, and in really "bully" style. General Mansfield complimented us highly and we have become his special pets. Of course we felt good. I tell you the Thirteenth are just gay.

August 27th, 1862.

. . . As yet we are in complete ignorance as to our future movements. To-day the regiment received one month's pay and we were told that an order would follow immediately for us to break camp and start for home, instead of which we have received one to "prepare rolls for muster and pay" on Sunday, but as that is one of the routine duties no significance is to be attached to it. We have a rumor to-day that ten regiments are to arrive here shortly and that upon their arrival we are to leave. So you see we are, as we doubtless should be, quite in the dark. Our time expires to-morrow noon. . . . Paying off has, of course, given us a lively time to-day, but the boys don't know what to do with their greenbacks. I got $200.10, and although paid early this morning I have it all yet. The men got $13 each — not as much as they were entitled to, but the Paymaster said he was told to pay them "enough to pay their debts to the niggers."

The regiment remained at Suffolk the time for which it was summoned and for which it was mustered in. Being then ordered back to Brooklyn the troops left Suffolk by a small steamer for Fortress Monroe, where they re-embarked on the steamer *Baltic* together with the Twenty-fifth Regiment N. Y. State Militia. Directly the troops were on board the steamer started, but during the afternoon she struck on Chincoteague Shoals, where she lay hard aground for thirty-six hours. During the first night a heavy storm came up and the severe pounding upon the bottom caused the ship to spring a leak. All hands set to work heaving coal overboard and working the pumps. The next afternoon several schooners came to the rescue and all the men were given the opportunity of leaving the steamer. The Twenty-fifth Regiment took advantage of the opportunity together with some of the Thirteenth, but most of the Brooklyn regiment stuck by the *Baltic*, and of Company G only one man left. On the second day the *Baltic* was floated and, although the trip was far from pleasant, she reached New York in safety.

IV

IN THE GETTYSBURG CAMPAIGN

EARLY in 1862 the Twenty-third Regiment N. G. S. N. Y. was organized, largely from the membership of the Thirteenth Regiment, and on the fifth of February, 1863, Lieutenant-Colonel Woodward of the old regiment was elected Lieutenant-Colonel of the new, which honor he accepted. On the twenty-third of the following month, the Colonel of the Thirteenth Regiment having resigned, Lieutenant-Colonel Woodward was elected to succeed him. Strong efforts were made to persuade Colonel Woodward to remain with the Twenty-third, but his inclination and his sense of duty led him to return to the regiment with which he had been so long associated and which he considered still needed his services. He at once set about improving the drill and discipline of the command. The condition of the Union campaign was not promising and it was apparent to military men that the services of the National Guard would shortly be needed again. At last this became a certainty. After the defeat of the Army of the Potomac, at Chancellorsville, General Lee's army moved northward, and on June fifteenth, 1863, entered Pennsylvania. General George W. Wingate, in his history of the occurrences in which the National Guard of New York took part, says, "At that time General Couch, the commander of the department of the Susquehanna, had, he states in his official report, less than two hundred and fifty organized troops for duty in his department, on June 16th, when the Confederate force entered Chambersburg, sixteen miles north of the Maryland line. . . . On June 15th Secretary Stanton appealed to Governor Seymour of New York, . . . asking him if he would not immediately forward twenty thousand militia as volunteers without bounty, or what number he could possibly raise. This appeal was supplemented by another from Governor Curtin of Pennsylvania to Governor Seymour,

stating that the enemy is now in Cumber-
land Valley in large forces, the danger is imminent, and urging him to forward all troops
to Harrisburg without delay. Orders to the
National Guard for their immediate departure
to the front were issued by Governor Seymour on the eighteenth of June, the day these
telegrams were received, and Governor Seymour at once telegraphed to the Secretary of
War that 'about twelve thousand men are now
on the move for Harrisburg, in good spirits
and well equipped.'"

Colonel Woodward had learned from experience that it is unwise to despatch a regiment
to the front insufficiently equipped. But on
the twentieth of June the Thirteenth started,
four hundred and ninety-six strong. This
was a smaller number than had left with it
on previous occasions; but many of the members who had accompanied the command in
1861 and 1862 had now enlisted in the volunteers, and many had gone into the Twenty-
third. During its march through the streets
the regiment was again saluted by the enthusiastic citizens in great numbers, and all

13

were sensible of the gravity of the situation and the perilous nature of the campaign. Without the heavy bounties such as were then being paid to volunteers, the men were hastening to confront the exultant veterans of Lee, who outnumbered by more than ten to one the force that could be gathered to arrest the rebel advance along the line of the Susquehanna until the Army of the Potomac could come up. To stimulate the zeal of the National Guard the War Department issued an order promising a medal of honor to every man of this emergency force, a medal such as is usually awarded only for distinguished service on a forlorn hope. The Thirteenth arrived at Harrisburg on the twenty-third of June, and the men were immediately set to work strengthening the improvised fortifications and clearing away the woods that might have concealed and sheltered the enemy. York was occupied by the rebel General Early on the twenty-second and the bridge across the river at that place was burned by its defenders. General Lee had ordered that Harrisburg should be attacked on the thirtieth.

General Jenkins, of Stonewall Jackson's division, made a reconnoissance of the works on the twenty-eighth, and on the following day General Ewell advanced to begin the attack. If it had been vigorously pressed there could, in view of the great disparity in numbers and the superiority of the rebel forces, have been but one result. Harrisburg must have fallen, the Union troops would have had difficulty in avoiding capture, and the victorious rebels, only a little more than a hundred miles from Elmira, would have absolutely commanded the railroad system of Pennsylvania, with Philadelphia easily at their mercy. The plucky stand made by the National Guard regiments checked the rebel advance just long enough to prevent such disasters and to enable the Army of the Potomac to catch up with Lee and compel him to call in all his forces and concentrate them upon Gettysburg. An intelligent critic declares that the handling of the National Guard contingent at this time by the brigadiers from New York was unskilful and inefficient. This also appears plain from Colonel Woodward's letters. The actions of the troops were, however, prompt, vigorous, and effective. During this campaign the filial spirit of Colonel Woodward was again manifested in letters to his father. The first, written from Fort Washington, Harrisburg, was dated the twenty-third of June.

DEAR FATHER,

I have been positively prevented from writing even a little except as required in the routine of business. The papers will have informed you that we are at present engaged in the defense of Harrisburg, being, together with the Twenty-third, encamped within a large earth-work named as in the heading of this letter. The works are located on the crown of a high hill which slopes toward the river on one side and the most beautiful valley in the world on the other. We lie on the steep slope toward the river. The tents are therefore uncomfortably slanting, and the men are obliged to dig their toe-nails in deep to keep themselves from sliding out of the tents at night. I have not got my tent up yet and the field and staff are now all in one hospital tent. I have my hands full as can be. The very first want I experienced was a horse. To-day I bought a very large one. . . . To-night thousands of people are flocking into the city, as the rebs are coming down upon us. At noon some twenty graybacks were brought in, having been captured about twenty miles out. Altogether things look like work. I have orders to be ready for the advance movement at a moment's notice.

Other letters follow.

IN CAMP AT FENWICK, June 29th, 1863.

DEAR FATHER,

I think I wrote you last on the twenty-fifth. That evening as we were eating supper General Hall rode up to my tent in much excitement and ordered me to have the " long roll beaten and that I get the men in line immediately, and to march right away." I asked him where we were to march to. He said to report at his headquarters. I inquired what the men were to carry. He answered that we were to go out some six or eight miles for picket duty. I accordingly assembled the

regiment, ordering each man to carry rubber and woolen blanket. This was done
promptly. I reported to General Hall and
he ordered me to march to this point. We
started at quarter-past eight in the evening,
marched nine miles, and arrived at 10:35. I
call that quick work, but we heard on the
route that Yates, who is in command here, was
getting pounded. On our arrival we were
much astonished to find the General comfortably in bed, entirely oblivious of our coming.
He did not know what to do with us. That
night we passed in a train of cars. The next
morning we had nothing to eat except what
we could get at the few farm-houses in the
neighborhood. My share was nix. At eleven
o'clock we were sent on the picket-line —
stayed there all day in a piece of woods.
Dinner was supplied, by the kindness of the
Twelfth Regiment, in small quantities. Supper was missing altogether. At four o'clock
Yates ordered me to Harrisburg to get our
tents and truck out. I rode down as fast as
the horse could go, impressed wagons, got the
goods together, and brought all that six wag-

ons could carry, being obliged to leave the knapsacks and the men's goods behind, for lack of transportation. Got back here at nine o'clock and found my men in line of battle on the edge of a piece of woods. At eleven o'clock a drenching rain from the northeast came on and continued all night and all the next day. Of course, being without shelter we were soon soaked. My tents were about a mile behind us. We passed the night wretchedly. In the morning I took the liberty of issuing the tents,. (shelter), to the men, and they pitched them in the woods. The ground being ankle deep in mud the tents improved our condition only as would an umbrella that of a man in a bath-tub with the shower-bath turned on. The rain continued incessantly until six o'clock, when it abated to a drizzle. Another uncomfortable night, except that in spite of everything we slept, being worn out. Large bonfires have been burning all day and were kept up all night. About eight o'clock I got the men all around me in a crowd and complimented them upon their good behavior. It is strange, but quite true, that not a man has absented himself or indulged in any grumbling during the whole time. I command a regiment of Mark Tapleys. The morning brought us evidences of a clearing-up. About ten o'clock the sun shone, and by sheer persuasion our most wise and able general, who had kept us in line of battle for forty hours, with the enemy as many miles away, consented to our going into camp. Our present location was selected and by noon we were comparatively comfortable. The day previous the knapsacks, overcoats, etc. of the men had arrived. They were, owing to the neglect of the officer I left in command while I was away scouting and mapping the country, indiscriminately scrambled for. Imagine the result. Every man, almost, has somebody else's clothes. My men spent the afternoon in drying and brushing up what they had left of them and at tattoo entered their tents hoping for a good night's rest. Again our most distinguished and accomplished general, Yates, got an idea into his head to do something for our comfort. At eleven and a half we were routed out and marched to headquarters, two hundred yards

away, and there we lay all night and observed
the companies being detached every few minutes for the various purposes which his inge-
nuity devised, one company being sent to
garrison an earthwork composed of six rail-
way-ties piled one on another, backed by thirteen sandbags. Another detachment of two
companies had to garrison a breastwork composed of a pile of stones on top of a hill nearly
as high as the moon and commanding a road
used by two farmers' wives as the nearest way
to get their milk and butter to the main road.
So high above the earth is it that were it
not for the attraction of gravitation I doubt
whether a bullet fired from the summit would
reach the plain below. At two o'clock A. M. I
was sent with two companies to obstruct a
road crossing the mountain at Miller's Gap.
A guide was furnished who was the same fellow that gave the information to the general
of the existence of the road. As the lower
parts of all the roads in the vicinity had been
obstructed we found it hard work to get
started on our mission but succeeded in getting around the obstructions. After laming

14

my horse in both hind feet so seriously as to render him entirely unserviceable we marched directly up the mountain side, when, finding the men unable to stand it longer, and having grave doubts as to the existence of the road and as to the guide's knowledge of the place, I halted the men and rode along alone with the man. After spending an hour in a fruitless search I gave the fellow a dose and returned to where I left the men. I found the poor fellows all fast asleep; got them up and back to headquarters at six o'clock. You will see that I was in the saddle all night. My poor horse's feet were all torn to pieces and good for nothing. At seven o'clock, finding the general was in bed and asleep, I took the responsibility of getting the regiment back into camp, where we spent the balance of the day, and, strange to say, we were all allowed to remain undisturbed. Thus you observe that we passed the nights of the twenty-fifth, twenty-sixth, and twenty-seventh without sleep and but partly fed. For new men coming from featherbeds this is too much to require, but in spite of it all I have not a man in the hospital and but very few cases needing medical assistance. I have stood it remarkably well, but I have not escaped entirely, having caught a terrible cold, which has got on my chest, and the coughing is very painful. To-day I am much better and able to attend to light duty.

I presume you are already in possession of as much news as to the whereabouts of the rebs as we are. It is my impression that a fight is very imminent and I have shaped everything to be in readiness for it. If they come here we shall all be gobbled, as we have not over fifteen hundred men, and our general appears to think it the height of prudence to scatter us as much as possible. I have not been able to give the men any drill, either by company or regiment, yet I have faith that they will make a good stand. We have news from Harrisburg this morning that the rebs are close upon that place, and as no trains have come up from there to-day I am inclined to believe that we are cut off. We, however, can easily get across the river and obtain a safe retreat unless they stretch in and destroy a bridge that is in front of us.

The outside of the letter bears this endorsement: "Lord! How we would appreciate our old Dutch General Webber. Militia generals are a nuisance."

CAMP CROOKE, FENWICK, PA.,
June 30th, 1863.

DEAR FATHER,

Up to the present time we are guiltless of having seen or heard the rebs, though last evening we heard very heavy firing at Harrisburg. We see by the papers of to-day that they were fighting there, but people from there say that the artillery were merely practising. . . . There are two railroad bridges across the river at this point, one of which is passable for infantry, the other but partially so. Sterret's Gap was a good entrance to this valley, and through it the rebs would have come a day or two since had it not been obstructed by blasting rocks and felling trees. Miller's and several other gaps in this valley have also been filled up, so that if they come they will have trouble to get in. However, it can be done. If they intend to attack Harrisburg from the front they will have a hard fight at the fort where we were first stationed. If they wish to get the city easier they can flank it by driving us out of this position. If they intend this last movement they must use cavalry in large numbers and skedaddle us or we shall burn the bridges. A few miles above here the river is fordable, but barely so. The troops here consist of the Fifth, Twelfth, Thirteenth, and Twenty-fourth New York, and a detachment of the Twenty-eighth Pennsylvania, besides two pieces of artillery. There is canonnading going on somewhere within ten miles of us now. It sounds, however, like drill practice.[1]

P. S., July 1st. A quiet night. We hear that the rebs are retreating. We expect orders to follow them up.

FORT WASHINGTON, HARRISBURG,
July 3d, 1863.

I think I wrote you last Monday evening, from Fenwick. We heard a good deal of fir-

---

[1] It was the fight at Oyster Point between Jenkins' advance and General Ewan's brigade, which consisted of the Twenty-second and Twenty-seventh Regiments National Guard of New York and Laud's battery.

ing that night from the direction of Sterret's
Gap and I was kept busy nearly all night.
Tuesday was a rainy day which I spent almost
entirely in my tent and asleep. Wednesday
was bright and clear. Cleaned up the camp
and had company drill and dress parade.
Had a good night's rest until eleven o'clock,
when we got orders to break camp and return to the fort at Bridgeport, which is opposite Harrisburg. At half-past twelve we
were under way. At half-past five or six we
were comfortably located in the tents of the
Twenty-third, which regiment had been ordered to go to Carlisle. This was lucky for
us, and last night we enjoyed a good night's
sleep. This morning we have cleaned camp
thoroughly and it bids fair to be a comfortable
place for some one to pass the night. I fear,
however, that we are not to be left in peace
for many hours together, and as it is clouding
up very rapidly I guess we shall have orders
to-night.

Up to noon to-day the Twenty-third had
not reached Carlisle but were pressing forward. I have sent a company (E) in light

marching order, well armed, to go through by
railroad. They may be away some time. It
will be their business to protect contrabands
repairing the track. . . .

P. S. Eleven o'clock P. M. Copy of order
this moment received.

HEADQUARTERS FIFTH BRIGADE, N. G. S. N. Y.,
FORT WASHINGTON, July 3d, 1863.
COLONEL :

You will have all the troops under your
command ready to march at 2 o'clock to-morrow morning. The troops will be in light
marching order with blankets and canteens
and haversacks, but without knapsacks. They
will take with them whatever rations you have
on hand. It is of the utmost moment that
the troops should be ready to the moment.

By order BRIGADIER-GENERAL HALL.

Now you know as much as I do. J. B. W.

IN THE MOUNTAINS, SOMEWHERE BETWEEN CARLISLE
AND GETTYSBURG, July 6th, 1863.
DEAR FATHER,

The last letter I wrote was from Camp at
Harrisburg. I copied an order just then re-

ceived. This is the result. We started punctually by railroad for Carlisle. They took our horses from us. Got to Carlisle half-past seven, left there half-past twelve. The men, having been fed by kind-hearted people, marched out in a terrific northeast rain three miles, halted at a big barn for a couple of hours, resumed the march, and kept it up until ten o'clock at night. Slept in the road, in the mud. Rained all night. I slept very well, never better. Resumed the march at nine o'clock the next morning. No grub. Halted at a little hamlet surrounding an iron forge. The men confiscated flour, mixed it with water, and baked on their plates. Started at two o'clock for a mountain pass. Marched four or five miles; laid in the woods all night. Still raining. Marched again at seven this morning and came about two miles to this place. Are now in a clearing surrounded by woods. I believe we are ten miles from Gettysburg. Rebels in great plenty during the night and this morning. Sent a good many to headquarters. All my baggage is with me. Items: zouave jacket, trousers, big boots, haversack, opera glass, and overcoat. No blankets. Was very sick when I left the forge. Am now well, never felt better in my life, hungry, wet as a rat; having forded a dozen streams boots hang tight to my legs, overcoat weighs fifty pounds. General Crooke is a brick: marched on foot with us all the way and shared our fortunes. The men are in good order and spirits; not one sick, but many foot-sore. Don't worry, we are all right. This [which was a mere scrap] is all the paper in the regiment. If I had more would write as long as we lay here.

WAYNESBURG, PA., July 9th, 1863.

I last wrote you on Monday the sixth at about noon. Immediately after finishing the letter we marched, the weather having cleared and the roads drying somewhat. Proceeded steadily until ten P. M., when we halted in a piece of woods and bivouacked, getting a shower-bath before morning. Marched about ten miles the next morning, (the seventh). Started at eight A. M., marched five miles to Chambersburg pike. Here we had one day's rations of hardtack served; killed a steer and

ate him. . . . Started the march again at three
P. M. and reached a place called Funkstown or
Altodale. We encamped on the outskirts of
the town, in a piece of woods. At ten P. M. it
commenced to rain again and it rained in
dead earnest, soaking us completely. A small
stream passing through the woods became
swollen and overflowed the camp, washing out
the fires and nearly drowning some of us before we woke up. The balance of the night
was very uncomfortable. The next morning,
(the eighth), the rain was still pouring until
about eleven o'clock, when it cleared up. At
noon resumed the march through mud, mire,
and fording swollen streams. At seven P. M.
reached this place, and are now in line of battle on the top of a high hill where a battery is
planted. The hill is crowned with woods and
we are on the skirts of the woods — a very
pleasant place, but water is very scarce. My
horse arrived last night and this morning the
Quartermaster has brought up my baggage. I
have therefore washed, brushed my hair, got
on clean socks, but I am without a clean shirt.
I will try to keep my baggage with me, but

may send it home or abandon it. Rebels were very plenty again last night and this morning: sent a lot of them to headquarters. Lee's entire army is said to be in front of us, but as I have not seen a paper since the third it would be folly for me to attempt to state where either party is. We have rumors that Lee has been routed, that Grant has Vicksburg, and that Dix is in Richmond. We are within a mile and a half of the rebel cavalry picket. It is believed, however, that they are retiring, in which case we are to follow them up. They have burned a bridge some distance in front of us, which must be rebuilt before we can get to them; so I hope for a day's rest. It is now six A. M. Plenty of men sore footed but none sick.

WAYNESBORO, PA., July 11th, 1863.

I intended to write a long letter, but five minutes ago, and while we were all preparing for brigade review, I received orders to get ready for the march. We are now within a very few miles of Lee's army, so we can't have much of a tramp unless we are to make a retrograde movement, which I presume is hardly supposable. To-day we have had an issue of rations, (half rations), being the first proper issue since the third of July. The men, of course, have eaten in the meantime, but only what they could beg or buy, which consisted of bread and apple-butter. We are in poor condition for the march. The last two days have been very pleasant, but to-night it is clouding up and intends, I presume, another rain-storm. To tell the truth, I prefer a march in the rain to the hot sun. I am still in first-rate health. I have a horse, not the one I bought, but still a most excellent one. The health of the regiment is not as good as it was, but it is not bad. It is hardly worth while to write me as our movements are very uncertain and rapid.

IN A SHELTER TENT AT CAVETOWN, THUNDER, LIGHTNING, AND RAIN, July 12th, 1864.

The day is dark and dreary, and the wind (and rain) is never weary, &c. . . . We left Waynesboro, that interesting spot, at six P. M., after having eaten our half rations. At eight o'clock we forded a stream called the Little

Antietam, the rebs having burned the bridge. The fire was still smoldering and we were close upon their heels. We kept jogging along until half-past ten P. M., when we filed up into a clover-field and bivouacked for the night. I had my shelter-tent, which I carry with me, and Dr. Ormiston, Dr. Pray, and myself passed the night in comfort. At four A. M. we were up and on the road again, and at twelve M. reached this place, having come most of the distance across lots. We went supperless to bed and were put on the march without a particle to eat. The consequence was that when I got here I had about seventy-five men with me, the balance being strewn along the road, overcome by the march without food. I halted in a clover-field alongside a brook and we are bivouacked here. It had been threatening rain all day and at two o'clock a frightful thunder-storm broke upon us. Fortunately my tent had been pitched, and I am in it with two others; but these shelter-tents are like umbrellas, they keep off only the heaviest part of a rain. They leak, and we have a little rainstorm inside, so we put our rubber blankets

around us and squat on the ground and let it
rain. The balance of our division is in bi-
vouac some half-mile from here, and orderlies
have been trotting here all the afternoon with
orders to move up to them, but as I have not
twenty men here I think I will wait. The balance are around the town getting, (buying or
stealing), grub. I don't blame the men, for we
must eat, and to do that we must obtain ma-
terials. The inhabitants are mainly very kind,
and I guess very few men have failed to get a
good feed since our arrival. There are some
few Secesh here, being the first we have come
across, and they are very uncivil. Some of
my best officers were used up, Bach among
them, and I have just heard that he is lying
in a field a couple of miles away from here,
without any shelter. I immediately sent two
of his men to bring him in. Our hospital
steward forages for me and the staff, and Dr.
Pray's man, Matthew, cooks for us; so we
never miss our three meals a day, except upon
the march, and not often then; so when I
speak of having eaten nothing I speak collec-
tively and not individually. To-day I have

eaten any quantity of bread and apple-butter, a heap better than nothing.

We have all sorts of rumors in camp about the place where Lee and the rebs are located. I know that they cannot be far away, for they have just left everywhere we have marched in. All the Brooklyn regiments except the Forty-seventh are here, and we are all growling about our treatment, but I suppose the "darned militia" are not worth anything anyhow. However, it does seem hard to make as many sacrifices as we have and then, when here, to be snubbed and maltreated. The three-years' troops who are here have everything they need. We have not a single wagon. Our men are obliged to carry along, between them, their cooking utensils, mess-pans, etc. I pack my horse's back full in order to transport what is necessary for myself, yet I have not a single change of clothes. All this I could stand if we had rations for the men. I can't and won't give them a single particle of extra work. In consequence we have no camp guard, and the men come and go as suits their own pleasure, but they behave well and I have no complaints to make about them. We have here a certain General Knipe, who was formerly a clerk at Harrisburg, a very gross sort of fellow, who appears to have a grudge against us Yorkers. He threatened in Harrisburg to give us——. We think he has succeeded. He says he will put us in a fight to see whether we have any pluck. Perhaps he will succeed in that. He struck one of our darkies yesterday with his riding-whip for being a little slow in entering the ford.

As the ground is wet, and nothing between it and my trousers, I feel a little moist like, so I think I will give over writing and go and stand with my back to the fire which is burning in fine style in front of my tent. Snake fences make good fire-wood. Here's the General and I must move.

BOONSBORO, July 14th, 1863.

Immediately after I closed my last letter we got on the march for another camp site, about half a mile away. Here we received the meat of a small steer and the proceeds of two barrels of flour that filled the men somewhat.

The next morning, (the thirteenth), we marched at eight o'clock, on the Smoketown road, but soon struck off on to the road for this place. The day was rainy. At noon we halted in a piece of woods and pitched the tents. It being promised that we were to receive rations we built fires to cook, but the grub did not come. At six o'clock we broke camp and got under way for Boonsboro. Halted at ten P. M., still raining, and bivouacked in a stony field. Here we found ourselves incorporated with the Army of the Potomac, and we were entirely surrounded with camp and signal fires. Early this morning I drew and obtained one and a half day's rations, which were issued to the men, and to-day all is quiet. At eleven o'clock we struck across country and marched about two miles to our present camp, which is two miles from Boonsboro on the Hagerstown road. Saw to-day's "Tribune," which was a great treat. This afternoon I rode into town and found cousin George, who was stopping at a hotel. I also came across a good many acquaintances who are in the army. To-morrow I shall try to find the Fifteenth Massa-

16

chusetts. I am told there are only about one
hundred of them left. I hope to find Harris
among them. The news to-night is that Lee
has got safely across the Potomac. From the
large amount of cheering in the regiments
about us I suppose the New York troops have
orders to leave for home to-morrow. I believe
we are to be allowed to march to Carlisle,
some sixty miles, and there take the cars.

Your affectionate son,

Jno. B. W.

P. S. Fifteenth. Am on horseback on the
road to Frederick and home.

This is the last of the war letters. There is
a telegram from Frederick, dated the sixteenth
of July, which reads as follows:

At Frederick. Will be detained several
days. Will telegraph again.

Another telegram came on the seventeenth,
merely saying,

At Baltimore on the way home.

The hardships of the regiment during this service were very great, and the Colonel's letters to his father distinctly specify several of the most important respects in which the welfare of the troops was neglected. The Brooklyn "Eagle" of July twentieth, reviewing the enlistment of the regiment, said:

They experienced a terribly rough time during their brief campaign, and, although not participating in any battles, did enough marching in mud up to their knees, and in a few instances in water up to the armpits, to make up in a measure for the lack of bullet exercise.

However, there is abundant evidence that the men themselves felt and recognized the fact that their commanding officer did all he possibly could to relieve the deplorable deficiencies of other departments. A member of the regiment, ("J. S. W."), writing to the "Eagle" under date of June twenty-ninth, declares: "Our Colonel takes good care of us and sees that we get everything possible."

This disposition to care for his men is shown in the official report of Colonel Woodward, dated the tenth of December, 1863, in which the service of the regiment in repelling the rebel invasion is succinctly described.

"Previous experience in the field," says the report, "of privations and sufferings caused to enlisted men by hurrying off a regiment half uniformed and equipped, and poorly supplied with medical and other stores, caused me in this instance to be more anxious to leave the city thoroughly supplied and equipped than to earn the distinction of being the first in departure reckless of the consequences which attended upon the honor."

Although the regiment had, since the outbreak of the rebellion, put in more than seven months of active field service, the moment they were back from their last enlistment they were called on to aid in suppressing the draft riots in New York. The local journals of July twentieth described the enthusiastic reception accorded to the returning soldiers, and the order to the Thirteenth for service in suppressing the riots is dated the twenty-first. In fact, it was because the Thirteenth was so well qualified for such work that it was sent home so expeditiously, and Colonel Woodward's effectiveness in riot duty was cordially recognized by the civil authorities. The regiment was not again called into the field, although at times it seemed likely that the Nation would again need its assistance. The Colonel devoted himself assiduously to the regular duties of his position, encouraging the filling up of the ranks, the selection of proper company officers, and the proper equipment and thorough instruction of the officers and men. While riding one day at the head of the Thirteenth, after a parade in which the regiment had made a particularly fine appearance, the thought occurred to him, as he himself stated to a friend long afterwards, that he had now done all he could for the regiment, and that he had better give place to some one else. Accordingly, on June sixteenth, 1866, he resigned his commission.

V

LATER SERVICE IN THE NATIONAL GUARD

FOR nearly three years Colonel Woodward was out of military life, but on the twenty-fourth of March, 1869, he was nominated by Governor Hoffman as Major-General commanding the Second Division, N. G. S. N. Y., an appointment which was promptly confirmed by the Senate. The division of which he thus assumed command consisted of the Fifth brigade, comprising the Thirteenth, Fourteenth, Fifteenth, and Twenty-eighth regiments and a troop of cavalry, and the Eleventh brigade, consisting of the Twenty-third, Thirty-second, and Forty-seventh regiments, a troop of cavalry and a howitzer battery, together with a division troop of cavalry and Batteries A and B. The previous management of the division had been very unsatisfactory. Its books and papers were not properly kept and there was a neglect of administration and responsibility, not only in the division but in the two brigades. General Woodward surrounded himself with a staff thoroughly qualified by military service and also by important and successful business experience. A regular headquarters night was established, when every staff officer was expected to attend. A representative from each brigade and regiment of the division was also required to be present and a detailed report from each organization was demanded. The reports were immediately discussed and whatever action was suitable was forthwith ordered, so that the entire business of all the organizations of the division was promptly concluded. A headquarters night was also established for the two brigades, the commanders and staff of which occupied rooms adjoining those of the Major-General. By this arrangement matters which formerly had occupied weeks, or had been altogether neglected, were disposed of in a few minutes, and official delays, which had justified serious complaints, entirely ceased as far as the Second Division was concerned.

General Woodward took an active and prominent part in the development of rifle practice in the National Guard of this State and in the country. He was one of the original members of the National Rifle Association and upon its organization was appointed its treasurer, a position which he held for many years. He was also a member of its range committee, and took the chief part in the laying out and construction of Creedmoor. The first shot which was fired at the range, to test the targets, was fired by George W. Wingate, who was then a colonel upon General Woodward's staff, and the General himself acted as marker. Before Creedmoor was ready for use General Woodward had taken steps to introduce systematic instruction in rifle practice in the various organizations composing his command. In his annual report for 1871 he urged the necessity of introducing the system into the Guard, and in January, 1874, he induced his friend Wingate, who was then secretary of the National Rifle Association, to accept a commission as Inspector on his staff for the purpose of instructing the officers and men of the division in this subject. He required the officers of his division to attend the lectures given by Colonel Wingate and in every possible way pushed the system among the troops.

On December thirty-first, 1874, General Woodward resigned the command of the division and the rank of Major-General to take the place of Inspector-General of the State, where he ranked as Brigadier-General, to which position he was appointed by Governor Tilden on January first, 1875. His relinquishment of his old command was a matter of regret to all the officers and men, who, under his firm and just rule, had greatly advanced in military effectiveness, and with whom he was extremely popular. The breaking up of his staff excited especially keen feeling, as the General and the members had become deeply attached to one another, so they determined to convert the membership into a fraternal society. To that end the following agreement was drawn and executed on the fourth of January:

17

The undersigned, who have composed the Staff of the Second Division, N. G. S. N. Y. since the twenty-fourth of March, 1869, hereby organize themselves in an association to be entitled

THE GENERAL WOODWARD STAFF,

and pledge themselves to assemble on the twenty-fifth day of March in each year for the purpose of dining together, except when such date shall fall upon Sunday, in which case such assemblage shall occur on the next succeeding day.

Signed by

John B. Woodward, Major-General.

Brigadier-General Henry Heath, Assistant-Adjutant-General.

Colonel Ira L. Beebe, Assistant-Adjutant-General.

Colonel Henry T. Chapman, Jr., Inspector.

Colonel George W. Wingate, Inspector.

Colonel W. H. H. Beebe, Chief of Artillery.

Colonel Henry L. Cranford, Engineer.

Colonel Henry J. Cullen, Jr., Judge-Advocate.

Colonel J. M. Homiston, Surgeon.

Lieutenant-Colonel John E. Fay, Ordnance Officer.

Lieutenant-Colonel C. P. Gulick, Quartermaster.

Lieutenant-Colonel Robert B. Woodward, Commissary of Subsistence.

Major Isaac F. Bissell, A. D. C.

Major Francis E. Dodge, A. D. C.

Captain H. H. Hogins, A. D. C.

Captain J. Milnor Decker, A. D. C.

These reunions were kept up, with lessening numbers, for twenty-one years, until the time of the General's decease, and in that year two of the ten survivors also died.

Upon assuming the new duties to which he had been called by Governor Tilden, General Woodward proceeded to apply to the entire National Guard of the State the methods that had proven successful in his administration of the Second Division. The experiences of the war had established a new and very high standard of efficiency for every military organization. The condition attained by the

various organizations of the National Guard
was supposed to be ascertained by the annual inspections. The fundamental difficulty
in the Guard at this time was that the inspections were in a military sense really no
inspections at all. The whole organization
was largely on paper and heavily over-offi-
cered. Although consisting of but twenty-
one thousand three hundred and thirty-eight
men, it was divided into eight divisions and
nineteen brigades. These in turn were composed of thirty regiments and thirteen battal-
ions of infantry, one regiment and nine troops
of cavalry, one battalion and ten batteries of
artillery. The Fourth Division at one time
consisted of a major-general, his full staff, a
brigadier-general and full staff, and one battalion of one hundred and eighty-three men,
so that when the whole division paraded the
relation between the number of commissioned
officers and privates was ridiculous. Each of
these divisions and brigades had on the staff
of the commanding officer an inspector who
inspected the various organizations belonging
to his own command. The duty of an inspec-

tor is one that requires special military quali-
fications, but these inspectors were, as a rule,
appointed for social and personal reasons. It
was the exception when one possessed military fitness for his duties. Each of them,
therefore, had a standard of efficiency quite independent of every other. Moreover, there
was a natural inclination on the part of each
to make the organization to which he belonged
appear as well as possible in the reports,
and for that reason they all were inclined to
gloss over deficiencies. General Woodward,
during the first years in his position as Inspector-General, established a new practice by
attending in person the various inspections of
the different organizations of the National
Guard of the State, so as to determine with
his own eyes their true condition. He also
exerted all his influence to bring about a
change in the method of all inspections. In
this he eventually succeeded, and upon his
suggestion a law was passed requiring the annual inspections to be made by officers in the
Inspector-General's department, in accordance
with the practice in the regular army, a rule

which is still continued. This was one of the most important reforms ever effected in the National Guard, and one to which the present high standard of the force is largely due.

General Woodward appointed as Assistant Inspectors Colonel John E. Fay and Major Thomas A. McGrath, who had previously served in his command, and thus for the first time general headquarters at Albany were fairly informed of the actual merits of the different organizations comprising the military force of the State.

This was a critical period in the history of the National Guard. The nation had passed through a long and bloody conflict and was tired of war. War stories were not read, war pictures could not be sold. The National Guard shared in the results of this reaction. A large number of its members had remained in the service from motives of patriotism and for a number of years had held themselves in readiness to respond to sudden orders for field service, three of which had been made in as many years. They had also done a great deal of guard and riot duty. All this had been at heavy sacrifices, and when the emergency was over many took their discharges. To those who had been daily reading in their newspapers the accounts of conflicts involving from ten thousand to one hundred thousand men on a side, militia service seemed of very little consequence. Recruits were therefore difficult to obtain and of those that enlisted many were undesirable. The best organizations had great difficulty in maintaining their strength and the poorer ones became demoralized. If it had not been for the increase of interest excited by the introduction of rifle practice it is difficult to say what might have been the result. The thorough inspections which General Woodward required disclosed which of the various organizations of the State were unable to stand the strain of the new requirements. Where it was possible to maintain an organization by fostering care every endeavor was made to do so. Where, however, it clearly appeared that it would waste the State's money to attempt to continue a regiment it was disbanded. The work of deciding upon the various disbandments which were made, of getting rid of incompetent and superfluous officers, and of raising the standard of those organizations which were retained, called for wisdom, discretion, patience, and firmness.

In the National Guard there was then, more even than there is at present, a political as well as a military side to be considered. Much depended upon the ability to obtain from the legislature the indispensable annual appropriations, and it would have been injudicious to antagonize that body. The idea of the necessity of military efficiency was new. Most of the major-generals had been appointed for political reasons, and many of the brigadiers were better politicians than soldiers. Consequently the authorities at Albany were exceedingly timid in regard to interfering with organizations or officers thought to possess political strength. General Woodward was tactful and sagacious in his measures for improving the Guard, and his consolidation of the force was done by degrees and with such obvious fairness and good judgment that but little resentment was excited. One method

which he pursued with great success, where
the condition of a regiment or battalion in a
smaller town or city was such as did not justify its continuance, was the organization in
its place of a "separate company" from the
best material of the disbanded regiment.
This company generally embraced the best
young men of the place, and the substitution
for an inefficient regiment of a strong, well-
drilled company, composed of first-class material, proved popular as well as effective. It
added greatly to the actual military strength
of the State, and these separate companies
have since done excellent service. If he had
been permitted by others in authority General
Woodward would have applied the pruning-
knife much more thoroughly than he did. As
it was, besides the substantial reform he actually accomplished, he prepared the way for
consolidations and disbandments which were
subsequently effected. The General also did
much to trace up the military property of the
State, which was scattered in many places,
and to establish regulations for properly car-
ing and accounting for it.

18

Immediately upon General Woodward's appointment as Inspector-General he determined to promote throughout the entire National Guard the rifle practice he had so successfully introduced in the Second Division. Supervision of rifle practice was at that time one of the Inspector-General's duties, under an act which had been passed the preceding year, but nothing of any consequence had been accomplished. General Woodward tendered the position of General Inspector of rifle practice to George W. Wingate, who accepted the position, and thereafter the General did everything in his power to assist that officer in his special work. General Wingate states that it is almost entirely owing to the constant support of General Woodward, not only at the time when rifle practice was directly under the supervision of the Inspector-General, but subsequently, when it was made into an independent department, that the new movement attained such success that the National Guard of New York decidedly surpassed the regular army in effectiveness with the rifle.

When Governor Tilden retired from office

his successor, Governor Robinson, reappointed General Woodward Inspector-General. It was during the incumbency of Governor Robinson that the riots broke out along the line of the Erie Railway which necessitated calling out the National Guard on the twenty-ninth of June, 1877. The entire duty of the collection and disposition of the force and the suppression of the disorder was conferred upon the Inspector-General. In this matter General Woodward showed intimate knowledge of the proper forces to be brought into service, great executive ability in assembling and handling them, firmness in dealing with the elements of disorder, and fine discretion in avoiding embarrassing negotiations in which both parties to the great strike endeavored to involve him. So sudden and unexpected was the appearance of the National Guard at Hornellsville and other points where the disorder had broken out, and so stunning was the arrest of ringleaders who were counseling violence, that the thousands of men who had gathered, intent on mischief, almost immediately abandoned their unlawful projects. General Woodward's official report, dated the third of July, says, "When it was learned that the troops were actually on the way and would soon be on the ground several classes of employees sent formal notice to the General Superintendent of the railroad that they would continue to perform their duties under the reduction of pay which had been ordered, and gave assurances which were deemed satisfactory that no breach of the peace would occur." Thereupon the military forces were dismissed and returned to their homes. It is obvious that although the prompt action of Governor Robinson in ordering out the troops, and the vigorous and skilful dispositions of General Woodward in maintaining order at Hornellsville, where the trouble began, entirely suppressed the outbreak, a feeling of bitter disappointment remained in the minds of thousands of railway employees at many points; for it was only about three weeks afterward when Governor Robinson again telegraphed to General Woodward, "Riots have broken out at Hornellsville. Please proceed to that point at once." Gen-

eral Woodward, in his report of the military
movements on this occasion, dated the twenty-
seventh of July, 1877, states that he received
this telegram at his office in New York at
half-past ten o'clock on the morning of Saturday, July twenty-first. On the same day a
regiment of the National Guard was ordered
to proceed to Hornellsville at once, well supplied with bullet cartridges. The official order
to General Woodward said, "You will have
the direction of the movements of the troops
as before." General Woodward was soon on
the way to the scene of disorder. The General's official report goes on to say: "At Elmira His Excellency the Commander-in-Chief
entered the train and gave verbal instructions
to locate sufficient force at Hornellsville to
insure success, leaving me full discretion to
select such commands as would in my judgment be the most efficient." Before the trouble was over regiments had been called out
from all over the State, and so swiftly did
they appear, in such impressive numbers, and
so admirable was their disposition and so
prompt their movements, that, although the

riots extended from one end of the State to the other, and notwithstanding the fact that the disorderly elements were much better organized than the rioters who wrought such havoc at Pittsburg and for some time succeeded in defying the militia of Pennsylvania, the thousands of turbulent men were dispersed and the whole affair was over in less than a week, and on the twenty-sixth of July, at three o'clock in the morning, General Woodward notified the Governor that he believed it prudent to allow the military forces to be relieved. On the same day the Governor telegraphed as follows:

ALBANY, July 26th.

GENERAL JOHN B. WOODWARD,

I have just received your telegram. I congratulate you upon your success. Accept for yourself and the gallant men of your command the thanks of the Empire State. You may relieve the different regiments whenever in your discretion it seems prudent to do so.

L. ROBINSON,
Governor & Commander-in-Chief.

After paying generous tributes to the Guard and to several officers who had large opportunities for distinguishing themselves General Woodward closes his report as follows: " It is proper for me to report that I took no part whatever in the conferences with the strikers. . . . At the same time I feel that the National Guard rendered a most valuable service to the State, and that their presence saved the County of Steuben the cost of the destruction of many millions of dollars of valuable property." This estimate of the value of the service rendered is fully justified by a consideration of the damage done at Pittsburg.

In April, 1879, Governor Robinson appointed General Woodward Adjutant-General of the State. His duties in this position took him away from his business a great deal and required him to spend some days of every week in Albany. The theory of the constitution of the State is that the Governor is Commander-in-Chief of its military forces, but as very few governors have ever had any military knowledge or experience, the practice of the constitutional commander-in-chief is to

select for the position of Adjutant-General
a person thoroughly qualified to take actual
command. Therefore General Woodward had
now become in fact the commander of the National Guard of the Empire State. The exer-
tions he had made while Inspector-General to
improve all branches of the service were now
resumed with redoubled energy and enthusiasm. The measures he inaugurated and enforced show that, while he was not oblivious
of the distinctions between a militia force
composed of citizens whose main time is devoted to their usual vocations and a body of
regular troops who have given up all other
callings and enlisted for military service alone,
he proposed to have every member of the
National Guard understand and fully realize
that service in the Guard was a serious matter imposing grave responsibilities and involving discipline, subordination, and obedi-
ence to officers. Some of the measures he
enforced seemed to many almost too severe
for a body of citizen soldiery, but before the
expiration of his term of office his wisdom was
universally conceded; and long after it was

the consensus of testimony on the part of those in positions to intelligently judge the matter that General Woodward had been of more value to the State in matters relating to the National Guard than any other man who had ever been associated with the military branch of the government. Indeed, even now this fact is more than a tradition and is recognized by those who were familiar with matters at the time of General Woodward's service and who have continued to take an interest in the Guard.

One of the last reforms effected during the General's command was in the State Military Association. This was an organization consisting of the officers of the National Guard of the State. It held an annual meeting at Albany for the purpose of discussing matters affecting the interests of the Guard. Theoretically it was valuable; practically it was not. Its constitution was democratic, not military. Every officer who chose to attend its convention was at liberty to do so; at its meetings a second-lieutenant stood upon the same footing as a major-general; and if a sin-

19

gle organization chose to send up a sufficient
number of officers as delegates it might domi-
nate the proceedings. In point of fact the
attendance was largely due to the custom of
various Adjutant-Generals of holding recep-
tions to the officers of the National Guard
throughout the State. General Woodward
had been president of the Association and was
thoroughly familiar with its defects. He was
equally sure of its having possibilities of usefulness. Mainly through his influence the
constitution of the Association was amended
so that it was made up of delegates appointed
by the different organizations upon a plan
which gave each its proper representation,
and as the consideration of military questions
became the chief purpose of the conventions
the delegates were selected for their fitness to
intelligently participate in the discussions, and
thus for the first time the organization exercised a salutary influence.

General Woodward held the position of Adjutant-General until, by the expiration of Governor Robinson's term of office, on the thirty-
first of December, 1879, his own term also

expired. Governor Cleveland subsequently
invited General Woodward to accept the
office of Adjutant-General, but by that time
he had become so much engrossed in civil
pursuits, and he had already given so much
of himself to military service, that he felt
justified in declining the honor. Therefore
on the expiration of his term as Chief of
Staff to Governor Robinson his official relation to the military force of the State termi-
nated. He continued to take a deep interest
in the affairs of the Guard, and his experience
and sound judgment were often consulted by
commanding officers. He was always especially concerned for the welfare of the Brooklyn
regiments, and retained to the last a warm
affection for the Thirteenth. If measures
of discipline were considered, both officers
and men were accustomed to go to the old
commander of the regiment for that good-
tempered counsel which never failed to find
the most amicable and yet soldierly way out
of embarrassing conditions. When concerts,
fairs, and exhibitions were undertaken for the
benefit of the regiment General Woodward was

always the first and most generous contributor and patron. It is scarcely an exaggeration to say that for many of the veterans who had seen active service under him, and for their families, he conducted, up to the time of his decease, a pension bureau of which he alone and the recipients of his benefactions had knowledge. Occasionally the gratitude of some old soldier, or of some member of a soldier's family, disclosed, what the General's friends had always suspected, that he never refused aid to the needy and deserving and that his contributions in this way amounted to very large sums.

The military branch of the government of New York State has comprised on its official roster many men of eminence and distinction. None of them possessed genuine military ability superior to that displayed by John B. Woodward. He held the highest trusts, and it may safely be asserted that in the entire history of the service no man has been of more real and lasting benefit to the force.

VI

ALTHOUGH General Woodward's military service was now ended he was still a young man, and the abundance of his energy and public spirit was at once, and always after, freely given in the support of all causes that enlisted the interest of good citizens, and was especially potent in all movements for the amelioration of the conditions of life in Brooklyn. Mr. A. Augustus Healy, who succeeded General Woodward as President of the Brooklyn Institute of Arts and Sciences, said, in a public address, " He was a thorough Brooklynite, heartily loyal to the city and remarkable among men for the readiness and cheerfulness with which he spent his energy and time and means in promoting movements which he believed for the public good. This continued throughout his life. He was never weary in

well doing. His devotion to the public welfare
and his activity in advancing it sprang from
a strong and generous impulse innate in the
man. . . . Men often act from mixed motives
while doing praiseworthy acts; General Woodward seemed animated wholly and singly by a
desire, which was almost a passion with him,
to promote those things which should make
for the welfare of all the people. He was more
fully and genuinely, I think, than any other
man I have ever known, a public-spirited citizen. . . . So far as my observation extends we
have never had a man who, during the whole
period of his life, was so genuinely, continuously, and disinterestedly public-spirited as
was General Woodward."

The only public office carrying salary or
emolument which he ever held was that of
President of the Department of City Works,
to which he was appointed by Mayor Hunter
early in 1875, and this he resigned before the
close of that year. Although he was extremely active in all associations undertaking
to affect the affairs of the city, he held no
other official position for many years. In

politics he chose the Democratic party as most nearly representing his own views and principles, but in local matters he was always independent. In affairs where men were not divided by political sentiments it was so natural to expect his support, and his co-operation was so freely and so often given, that it seldom occurred to any one to keep a record of services he rendered in such matters, and it is therefore impossible to present an adequate statement of his activities in civil life. There are, however, records of many instances where he was useful and in most of which he was a leader. The first plans for an elevated railroad in Fulton Street were by judicial action referred to a commission of citizens for careful consideration, and General Woodward was appointed on this commission. The result of this reference was a condemnation of the original plans, and, therefore, a substitution of others less injurious to the thoroughfare and the abutting property. Subsequently he was appointed on a commission to appraise the damages to the property caused by the building of the elevated structure and the

operation of the railroad. In 1872 he was one
of a committee of citizens organized for the
purpose of endeavoring to secure reforms in
the municipal government. The special object
of distrust was a department called the Water
Board. The General served on a sub-committee for examining the books and accounts of
that department. Probably he undertook his
task with a presumption that affairs in the department were not altogether as they should
be, but the natural and undeviating purpose
to deal justly led to his reporting that, so far
as the books and accounts were concerned,
they were correct in form and unassailable.
This report was received with disappointment by those who were more anxious to find
evidence in support of their preconceived
convictions than to be just to those who were
under public suspicion, but the report of the
sub-committee was evidently accepted as con-
clusive by the community. In 1880 he united
in the civil service reform movement and in
1883 was elected one of the vice-presidents of
the Brooklyn association organized to promote
that cause, which office he held until his death.

The secretary of the association, in a letter, says, "I remember that in early years he was often the only one of the vice-presidents present at meetings of the executive committee. I always found him interested and sympathetic with our work." In 1885 he was appointed by Governor Hill member of a commission to investigate charges against the management of Greenwood Cemetery, his associate commissioners being Mr. Samuel D. Babcock and Mr. Spencer Trask. On the twenty-eighth of April the commission made a report vindicating the management.

In 1883 a number of the most intelligent and public-spirited men of the city began a movement which resulted, early the next year, in the organization of "The Brooklyn Citizens' League," the main purpose of which was "permanently to secure non-partizan municipal government for Brooklyn." Numerous meetings were held to inculcate that teaching in various sections of the city, and much deference was paid to the League, in the autumn of 1884, by the local nominating conventions of both the national parties. The League pro-

20

posed several timely reforms in the government of the city and county, and originated bills abolishing the costly fee system that prevailed in the offices of the County Register and the Sheriff. These bills were actively supported before legislative committees, and one of them was passed by both houses of the legislature, but afterwards encountered the veto of the Governor. For some years the League gave special care to all bills affecting Brooklyn pending in the State legislature, supporting those that were good, opposing those that were bad, and laboring in a most practical way for the amendment of those that were not altogether bad and that were susceptible of being made of public benefit. A gentleman who has held high official position in the city government, and who was one of the most influential members of the Citizens' League, is authority for the statement that this movement really originated with General Woodward and that he was the first person who at that time perceived and asserted the desirability of separating municipal affairs from national politics. This, however, was not the General's first demonstration of political independence and civic courage, for he had opposed the nominees of his own party and zealously supported the candidacy of Seth Low in both that gentleman's successful contests for the mayoralty.

General Woodward's public spirit and aspirations for improvement in the municipal government were most conspicuously displayed in the fall of 1885. The nominations for city officers made by the regular conventions of the Republican and Democratic parties were, either in the character of the nominees or the circumstances that led to their nominations, such as to convince observant men that the election of either candidate for mayor would result in unsatisfactory administration. Many citizens felt that they could not vote for either candidate and that they ought to nominate a man who should be in character and environment free from the criticisms applicable to the nominees of the two national party organizations. Having been one of the earliest, if not indeed the first, advocate of non-partizanship, and as most sat-

isfactorily representing the sentiment for reform, General Woodward was selected. He
was extremely reluctant to become a candidate and accepted only upon being persuaded
by many of his friends that he was the most
conspicuously fit man to stand for the principles he had long advocated. His letter ac-
cepting the nomination tendered him under
these circumstances was a model and a com-
pendium of the right view of the duties of a
mayor of Brooklyn at the time of this candidacy. It was lucid and luminous. It went into
a discussion of the matters that were exciting special attention, and the keynote of the
whole communication was contained in the
following passage: "My belief is fixed that national politics have no proper place in matters
of mere municipal concern. The control of
business and the administration of a city
should be in its own citizens, and our State
Constitution should be so amended as to free
each city from interference or dictation at the
State capital. When each citizen clearly understands that he must get good government
for Brooklyn by his own work at the polls of

Brooklyn, and that no relief can be obtained from Albany, good local government will be permanently secured." The General's brief addresses delivered in many parts of the city were full of a lofty civic patriotism. At one of the meetings the General made a speech which may be quoted as fairly stating his own position and his relation to the canvass. It is as follows: "Fellow-Citizens: I hardly know how to commence at all. Here is the city of my birth. I have never known any home but Brooklyn, and here I hope to end my days. From the hour of my birth till now I never had ambition to be a leader among men or take official position, but when more than one thousand of my fellow-citizens called me to take this nomination I felt the duty of my citizenship to be that I should answer the call. In this spirit alone I enter the canvass. (Applause.) I don't pose as a reformer or present unusual claims for your votes. I appear as a plain citizen, before my fellow citizens, and if you see fit to elect me as your mayor my platform shall be to work for Brooklyn first, last, and all the time. (Applause.) I see no rea-

son why, in the management of the city government, any of our employees should be
turned adrift and a new set of men put in
their places by a change of administration.
If I am elected no man need feel any anxiety
for his place providing he is doing his duty
faithfully, but if he does not do his duty he
cannot summon friends enough to keep him
there. (Applause.) If I go into the mayoralty office it shall be to loyally enforce the
civil service rules. We tax ourselves to keep
our streets in order, to light them, and for a
thousand and one items. Why not spend our
money as we would in our private affairs?
The city should receive one hundred cents of
value for every dollar expended. I believe I
can be partizan in national matters, but what
does the coinage of silver have to do with
matters here? If I did not believe the city
could be run on non-partizan principles I
would never have appeared before you as a
candidate. I hope we shall go on this idea
and be successful. This movement means
non-partizanship in municipal affairs." The
General's candidacy was supported by the

Hon. Seth Low, who had twice filled the office of mayor with peculiar honor and distinction. Many of the most conspicuous Republicans were ranged on the same side, and perhaps the most impressive incident of the whole campaign was the resolution of the renowned Young Republican Club to support the candidacy of General Woodward. It is no disparagement of the masses whose votes were divided between the two great parties to say that the wisest and best men of both parties supported this independent candidacy, and although the brief period between his nomination and the day of election was insufficient for perfecting an organization for the General's support over the entire city, nearly fourteen thousand ballots were cast in his favor. He himself was neither surprised nor disappointed that he failed of election, but he was satisfied because he had been able to afford those who believed in his principle of non-partizanship in municipal government a candidate and a ticket to vote for. While his championship of the reform cause was hearty and earnest, the entire kindliness of his manner and his abstention from offensive personal attacks enabled him to avoid causing rankling wounds among his opponents, and it is scarcely too much to declare that within a week after the election he was the most popular man in the city.

Indeed, during the subsequent period of his life no movement for the improvement of commercial or social conditions in Brooklyn seemed completely organized until it had secured the support of General Woodward, not a difficult matter; and the same statement is true to a measurable extent of affairs in New York City. It would be little if any exaggeration to say that in these years there was no such movement in his own town to which he did not lend counsel and active participation, and that his capacities and generosity made him a leader in most of the affairs in which he was engaged.

On the occasion of the laying of the corner-stone of the Egyptian obelisk in Central Park he served as aid on the staff of the marshal of the imposing ceremonies. At that time there were many of his friends who had forgotten that he was a member of the ancient and honorable order of Free and Accepted Masons, but although he had ceased to be active in the order, he had continued to take an interest in its welfare. It was in June, 1857, that he was made a Mason in Benevolent Lodge No. 28 of New York. On the twenty-second of February in the next year he united with Phœnix Chapter No. 2, Royal Arch Masons. Subsequently he transferred his lodge membership to Brooklyn, uniting with Commonwealth No. 409, in January, 1859, in which lodge he continued during the rest of his life. For some time after uniting with the order he took an active part in its work, but, as just intimated, in later years he seldom did more than attend the meetings, although on more than one occasion he was summoned to assist in important functions.

When Brooklyn was preparing for suitable entertainment of the Society of the Army of the Potomac in 1884, on the occasion of its annual convocation, General Woodward was made secretary of the committee on behalf of the city and was treasurer of the fund raised. Preserved among his papers is a letter of the

21

Mayor expressing his own thanks for the General's services in that matter and communicating the formal vote of thanks of the Common Council. The gratitude of the veterans had been less formally but most cordially indicated.

In 1889, on General Woodward's birthday, a large meeting of the citizens of Brooklyn was held to express sympathy for the people of Johnstown, Pennsylvania, which city had just been almost entirely swept away by a flood. It was resolved to raise a fund for the relief of the sufferers. The Rev. T. DeWitt Talmage was elected president of the association for this purpose and General Woodward was elected treasurer. About ninety-six thousand dollars were raised in Brooklyn and were quickly expended in the most wise and careful manner.

When Christendom was aroused by the outrages committed upon the Armenian Christians, in 1895, and the leading men of Brooklyn united, not only for the purpose of expressing their abhorrence of the crimes, but also to contribute for the relief of the Armenians who had been spared from murder, General Wood-

ward was again elected treasurer of the funds
collected among his fellow-citizens.

It has fallen to the lot of few, perhaps of
none, to be able to do so much as General
Woodward did toward the cultivation of a
taste for art, and to popularize art, in the city
of Brooklyn. Although he had no especial
eminence in any department of criticism, and
while he was not a patron, as that term is
applied to buyers, he was fond of art and was
appreciative and discriminating in his observation. He had traveled extensively in Europe, thereby enlarging his knowledge and
improving his taste, and wherever he went his
thoughts reverted to his native city and his
desire was that Brooklyn should become a
center of knowledge and of culture in the arts.
For years he had experienced delight in his
membership in the Rembrandt Club, which
has done so much for art in Brooklyn. He
was also a member of the Brooklyn Art Association and for several years was its President.
Partly as a lover of art, partly because it grat-
ified him to contribute toward any measure
for the decoration of his city, partly on ac-

count of the satisfaction it afforded him to
aid in commemorating the virtues of men who
had been useful in the community, he was
especially active in promoting the erection of
monuments to those who had been illustrious
in their times. When a citizen presented a
bust of Washington Irving to the city General
Woodward was chairman of the committee of
arrangements at the unveiling of the bust in
Prospect Park. He was one of the leaders of
the popular movement for the erection of the
bronze memorial of Henry Ward Beecher. He
was chairman of the executive committee of
citizens who placed the bronze statue of the
Hon. J. S. T. Stranahan in Prospect Park, and
was treasurer of the funds expended in that
affair. It was solely due to his early appreciation of the merits of Frederick MacMonnies,
and to his tactful insistence, that this brilliant
man received the commission for the Stranahan statue. It must have been a peculiar satisfaction to General Woodward, and it was
certainly a vindication of his recommendation
of an artist, that, when calling to order the
people who had assembled to witness the un-

veiling of the statue, the General was able to make the first public announcement that the French Salon had conferred upon Mr. Mac-Monnies the gold medal of honor for his artistic success in this work. Later General Woodward took a leading part, if not the leading part, in the measures which resulted in a commission being given to Mr. MacMonnies for an equestrian statue of Henry W. Slocum, one of the most successful generals in the war for the Union, and perhaps the most eminent soldier of all those who went out from Brooklyn.

After the canvass of 1885 General Woodward was not again a candidate for the suffrages of the people, but when it seemed to be his duty he at times accepted public office, to which he was often called by appointment, in the hope of being thus of the greatest possible service to his fellow-townsmen. In June, 1888, Mayor Chapin made him President of the Department of Parks. In that office he displayed to an eminent degree the best sentiments and the highest talents of an administrator of municipal affairs. Prospect Park, not through the fault of those in its charge, but owing to insufficient appropriations, had for years been falling into disorder, and the small parks of the city were in even a worse plight. General Woodward took especial pains with the small parks and succeeded in having them brought back to conditions of repair and attractiveness. Mainly through his own direct efforts the working force of Prospect Park was changed, reorganized, and greatly improved in efficiency, and during his presidency some of the most substantial and important adornments of that park which are now the pride of the city were begun. At that time the park commission consisted of eight members. General Woodward lent his support to a proposal for legislating the commission out of existence and creating a commission of only three members in its stead. After the enactment of such a measure the General was appointed by Mayor Chapin one of the three commissioners, an appointment which he declined to accept, not from unwillingness to serve the city but for personal reasons creditable to his good faith and honor.

In 1892 General Woodward was appointed by Mayor Boody member of a commission to lay out a parkway along the shore of The Narrows and the Bay of New York, and at the first meeting of that commission he was unanimously, and as a matter of course, elected its president. He evinced his customary zeal, tact, intelligence, energy, and good taste in the performance of his duties on this commission. The statute under which the commission was proceeding was not entirely satisfactory to the friends of the project, and in 1884 a more ample enactment was secured which necessitated the appointment of a new commission. By this time another mayor was in office, but, appreciating at its true value the service of the men appointed by his predecessor, he reappointed the five commissioners, adding two to complete the number required by the later statute. The political complexion of the city government having changed, and because another member of the commission had been active in promoting the passage of the legislation required, General Woodward, with characteristic magnanimity,

decided that it would be inexpedient for him
to retain the presidency. He was earnest and
persistent in presenting his view of the matter, but after discussion, and after being
unanimously elected president of the new organization, he with his invariable good nature
consented to serve. The far-seeing wisdom
and the good taste of the commission have
never been questioned, although its report
involved for its carrying out the expenditure
of several millions of dollars. Nearly four
millions of dollars have now been paid merely
for the acquisition of property comprised
within the borders of the parkway designed
while the General was living. When the report
which explained this design was received by
Mayor Schieren, who had appointed the lat-
est commission, he wrote a letter to General
Woodward thanking him for the very satisfactory treatment of the enterprise. Pursuant
to a provision of the statute a public meeting
was held in the City Hall at which all citizens
having objections to the report were invited
to attend and state the grounds of their objections. A large number of people were

present. Indeed, so numerous was the attendance that it was found necessary to adjourn from the rooms in which the meeting had first been called and to repair to the chamber of the Board of Aldermen. As citizen after citizen arose to speak, the Mayor, who was presiding, was compelled to call one after another to order and to remind those present that the meeting was not held to hear expressions favorable to the report but to consider objections. Finally, as no objections were presented, he declared the meeting dissolved. There have been subsequent and even more impressive demonstrations of the high popularity of the Shore Road in Brooklyn.

In 1895 it was determined by the responsible officials of Brooklyn to enlarge the city's system of parks, which at that time comprised less area in proportion to the population than the parks of any other city of importance in the United States. The extension of the parks by the acquisition of new lands was certain to involve the expenditure of several millions of dollars, and therefore required the wisest and most careful discretion. The legal power for

22

the acquisition was vested in the Park Commissioner, Mr. Frank Squier, but that official concurred with the Mayor in desiring the coöperation and approval of other citizens, and upon invitation General Woodward accepted service upon an advisory committee designated to assist the Park Commissioner in choosing such sites as should be most available and suitable. The coöperation of this committee and the Park Commissioner led to the purchase of more than double as many acres as the city formerly owned, and brought into the city's system Forest Park, Dyker Beach Park, Lincoln Terrace, Canarsie Beach, and several small pleasure-grounds. These instances of official action or of unofficial coöperation in matters of public concern are sufficient to indicate a versatile mind and a beneficent activity, but they are altogether inadequate to create a just impression of the unique eminence of this man. A stranger with no other sources of knowledge of the subject would fail to perceive how General Woodward came to be regarded as "in recent years the most useful citizen of Brooklyn," yet

when the memorial of one of the public associations to which he belonged made that
declaration, the fact was at once, by common
consent and without hesitation, universally
recognized by his contemporaries.

VII

ASSOCIATION WITH THE BROOKLYN INSTITUTE

GENERAL WOODWARD'S most important and effective work in promoting education and culture in Brooklyn was done through his association with the Brooklyn Institute of Arts and Sciences, which was at one time known as the Graham Institute. His family had been intimately associated with the Institute for upward of half a century. His uncle, George Woodward, who came to this country in 1819, was a naturalist and a large collector in zoölogy and botany along the Atlantic Coast, and in 1846 was elected a member of a committee of five to take charge of the natural history collections of the Institute and to promote its scientific interests. The General's father, Thomas Woodward, was also a member of the Institute, and on the

twelfth of January, 1852, was elected to the
Board of Directors, on which he served continuously until September, 1869. During this
period he was a member of some of the most
active committees of the board and was quite
zealous in the work. No director was more
constant and regular in attendance upon the
meetings of the board or more interested in
the welfare of the library and the development
of the scientific collections. General Woodward's own relations to the Institute began in
his early childhood, when he commenced taking books from the youths' free library. He
continued one of its readers for more than a
quarter of a century. When his father was
first elected director John B. Woodward became especially interested in promoting the
circulation of the library. His name appears
for the first time on the records of the Board
of Directors under date of January seventeenth, 1852, when he was appointed assistant
librarian, but long before this he had frequently gone with his father to listen to the
evening lectures. In his later years he was
in the habit of recalling with a great deal of

pleasure his experiences in giving out books
in the old library in the Washington street
building, and he delighted in memories of the
young people who were readers at that time,
with some of whom he formed friendships
which endured until his decease. On the fourteenth of January, 1867, he was first elected a
member of the Board of Directors, a membership to which he was continuously reëlected
in each succeeding year of his life. In 1887
the Institute, which had been in a declining
state, was put upon a more encouraging basis.
Its supporters having raised fifteen thousand
dollars by subscription, with which to remodel
and enlarge the building and to provide studio
rooms for artists, General Woodward served
on the committee which had charge of the
entire matter. From the beginning of his directorate he acted on the most important two
standing committees, those on library and on
scientific work. On the second day of May,
1870, he was elected secretary of the Board
of Directors, to which position he was an-
nually reëlected until 1878, when he succeeded
Mr. William Everdell as president. At the

end of a year he relinquished the presidency
in order to secure the election of General
Jesse C. Smith. The retirement of General
Woodward was characteristic of the man. He
could work quite as zealously in the ranks as
in command, and if it seemed to him that
another could do more effective service as
leader he was always willing to contribute
toward the promotion of that other and was
most active in conferring and supporting
such leadership. General Woodward again
accepted the position of secretary, and in
May, 1887, when General Smith, owing to advanced years and ill health, retired from the
presidency, General Woodward was again
elected to that position. Among the thousands who are now members of this great and
popular association probably very few know
that it is scarcely more than ten years since it
was a serious question as to whether it would
be possible to continue the Institute. A debt
had been contracted, when the Washington
street building was remodeled, which proved
to be an intolerable burden, and although
General Woodward was a determined, cour-

ageous, and hopeful man, in 1886 he was half
disposed to favor merging the Institute with
the Union for Christian Work. While con-
sulting with persons in New York who were
professionally engaged in work similar to that
comprised in the plans of the Institute he
heard of Franklin W. Hooper, who was at that
time professor of chemistry and geology in
the Adelphi College, and whose fitness to lead
in active efforts for reviving the Institute
was highly commended. He induced Professor Hooper to become interested in the
matter, and in May, 1887, the latter was
elected to the Board of Directors. At that
time General Smith, who was president, appointed as a committee on scientific work Professor Hooper, General Woodward, and his
brother, Colonel Robert B. Woodward. In
the autumn of 1887 this committee had frequent meetings and its members consulted
many persons in other cities whose advice and
counsel were likely to be of service in suggest-
ing useful and feasible measures. In that
same year, while General Woodward was still
secretary of the Board, he had the pleasure of

seeing the last dollar of indebtedness of the Institute paid off. He now became extremely desirous that the work of the Institute should be broadened in its scope and that it should become an active practical educational factor in the community. In December the special committee met in the parlor of General Woodward's house, when elaborate plans of reorganization and future work were presented by the chairman and were earnestly discussed for several hours. The committee entered heartily into the spirit of the new plans and from that evening until the time of his death the General gave unabated and enthusiastic aid in developing and executing those measures. When the committee reported to the Board of Directors General Woodward cogently and convincingly advocated the report and moved that the trustees invite the coöperation of scientific men and societies in Brooklyn. He presided at the first assemblage of representatives of the scientific institutions of Brooklyn and New York, held January twenty-eighth, 1888, before whom the methods of reorganization and enlargement of the Institute were

23

explained, and again, on Saturday evening the eleventh of February, he presided when thirty-six persons agreed to form an associate membership and to coöperate with the Board of Directors for the more effective carrying out of the provisions of the new organization. During the presidency of General Woodward, from 1887 to 1895 inclusive, the membership of the Institute was increased from eighty-two to three thousand seven hundred, the number of public lectures from eighteen to four hundred and ninety-six, the number of special meetings and class exercises from sixty to two thousand one hundred and twenty-five, and the annual attendance at the various gatherings of the Institute, which was six thousand nine hundred at the beginning of his presidency, had before its termination increased to over two hundred and eighteen thousand. In a published report of an interview General Woodward is quoted as saying, "It was in 1887 that I became president for the second time and was able to see plans for the Institute adopted and carried out. . . . We had struggled with a debt of fourteen thousand dollars, which was a source of endless embarrassment. On account of it the Institute had been practically lifeless for twenty years. Now see what we have — an endowment fund of more than two hundred thousand dollars in as good securities as can be found in Brooklyn and the city ready to issue bonds to the extent of three hundred thousand more in order to erect a museum building." General Woodward added, "And all this has been accomplished mainly through the efforts of Franklin W. Hooper." While the General was always generous in the bestowal of praise he was discriminating, but the accuracy of his award in this instance is questioned by Professor Hooper himself, who persists in declaring that the high position the Institute has attained is due very largely to the wisdom and energy and influence of General Woodward's leadership.

In December, 1888, plans for establishing museums of arts and sciences were approved by General Woodward at a meeting of the Council of the Institute, and were advocated by him in an address at a citizens' meeting over which he presided on the fifth of February, 1889. The city had for some years persisted in the policy of selling what were known as the Eastside Lands, but immediately previous to this time other counsels prevailed and it was determined to reserve that portion of these lands situated between Flatbush Avenue and the Eastern Parkway. General Woodward now advocated the enactment of a law authorizing the city to lease these lands to the Institute at nominal sums for museum and library sites. In 1890 the directors of the Institute desired a new charter from the Legislature, that should increase the power and scope of the corporation and change its name, and General Woodward brought many influential citizens to the support of the measure. It was he who proposed the legislation authorizing the city of Brooklyn to issue bonds with the proceeds of which the first section of the museum building might be erected. The coöperation of the city authorities, and the general public approval of these propositions, were largely the result of his own efforts and of the universal confidence felt in his trustworthiness and good sense. He lived to witness the interesting ceremonies at the laying of the corner-stone of the museum building of the Institute he had done so much to revive and advance, a building which will be one of the noblest structures in the United States, and will, it is conceded, be the model of the world for the purposes to which it is to be devoted. During his presidency, and unquestionably largely owing to his extraordinary capacity, the Institute from a moribund condition became an educational and refining factor of vast and perhaps unique importance. In 1895 General Woodward, much to the regret of every one of his associates, relinquished the presidency. At that time the death of one of his correspondents in the Argentine Republic necessitated a visit to South America; and in the spring of that year, perhaps realizing that the duties of his office were absorbing more of his time than he could justly take from his personal affairs and from his obligations to business associates, and perceiving that with its new development the Institute would require even

more time in the future, he determined on the
step which caused such deep regret and even
embarrassment.   He continued a director,
however, and after returning from his long
voyages he at once resumed his intimate association with the work of the Institute and
became, it may truly be said, its most important counselor.

VIII

IT was while General Woodward was trying to serve his neighbors that he caught the cold that led to his untimely death. A railway company was endeavoring to obtain from the city authorities permission to lay its tracks in Hicks Street or Henry Street, a project which the residents in the vicinity considered an injurious and unwarranted invasion of a quiet section of the town. A committee of the Board of Aldermen met at the City Hall on Thursday evening, the twenty-seventh of February, 1896, to consider the petition of the railway company and to listen to the remonstrants, with whom the General appeared. The Aldermanic chamber was uncomfortably warm and a window was opened which admitted an intensely cold draft directly upon the General. The next day he was evidently

ill, but he was not confined to his house and
went about his affairs as usual. On Monday
evening he attended a meeting of the Rembrandt Club. The following was the most aw-
ful day of the year, cold, dark, gloomy, stormy,
boisterous. General Woodward, however, had
always fairly rollicked in his consciousness of
physical vigor and general health, so that the
idea of its being imprudent for him to go out
in such weather, while suffering from a severe
cold, probably did not occur to him. He attended a meeting of the directors of the Third
National Bank of New York, at noon, but
shortly after he experienced a severe chill.
He went into the Down Town Club, of which
he had long been a member, and drank a cup
of hot tea, which for the moment seemed to
revive him. His brother urged the General to
let him call a cab, but he refused, because, he
said, it would alarm his wife to see him coming home during the day in such style. He
insisted upon going to his office, where he
spent some time, after which he started for
Brooklyn. Before he arrived at his house he
was seized with another chill. The ablest

physicians were at once summoned, but pneu-
monia quickly developed, and although every
resource and expedient of medical skill and
careful nursing was applied to the case, the
disease progressed rapidly and death ensued
a moment after midnight of Friday the sixth
of March, 1896.

The publication of the General's decease
was immediately followed by remarkable expressions of public and private appreciation
of his worth and of a sense of the irreparable
loss which the community had suffered. It
was the one topic of which men spoke as they
met in the streets and exchanges, at the clubs
where he was so well-known, and in all their
accustomed places. The press throughout the
country, and especially in New York State,
paid tribute to the character of a citizen
whose activities had for many years furnished
theme for its approving comment. In his
own city the evidences of sincere mourning
were extremely impressive and the editorial
remarks of the journals bore testimony to the
deep personal feeling of the writers. The
" Standard-Union " said:

24

He was one of the best representatives of an intelligent, public-spirited, and patriotic citizen who ever lived in this city.

The Brooklyn "Citizen" declared:

Looking back at the history of General Woodward as known to thousands of his fellow-citizens it is impossible to see how anything but good could be honestly written of him. He was an exemplary citizen, both in his domestic and business relations, and his public career left no blot on his name; not even the suspicion of selfishness.

The editorial of the Brooklyn "Eagle" was entitled "A Loss to Brooklyn." Its comprehensiveness and its felicity of phrase may justify giving it a place in this volume, and the greater part of it is therefore reprinted:

The death of John B. Woodward is a sad loss to citizenship, education, morality, clarified religion, friendship, and progress in Brooklyn. He was in the prime of life. He was on the right side of every public question here since he reached manhood. The people here have never decided adversely to the positions which he assumed, without being wrong. This could be said of very few Brooklynites. It can be confidently and truthfully said of him. Nevertheless he always knew that the people meant right even when they did not succeed in doing right. He tried his utmost to temper even their wrongful decisions with their highest intentions in making them. His object was to get for the government the right instrumentalities and out of even inferior instrumentalities the best possible results.

On the lines which create and divide parties he was a partizan. On those lines in State and in home affairs which concerned only the business conduct of public business he was an independent. Yet as an independent he was neither too good, nor was he hard to live with, nor as a partizan was he rancorous, opinionated, or intolerant. . . . His learning illuminated, humanized, ameliorated, and refined his business sense. That sense strengthened, organized, and made practically serviceable the learning of the man.

We presume that those who were thrown
into association with him were mainly impressed with his unusual executive gifts. . . .
Not only was he a model citizen, but he was a
patriotic and valiant soldier. He sympathized
with the national military spirit in his teens.
He upheld the cause of the Union and of freedom in the war. He was the effective commanding general of the entire force of the
State of New York in peace, bringing the
equipment and housing of our National Guard
before the public attention in a way which has
been realized by the merited and rewarding
results of to-day. In civil life he was a wise
administrator, a conscientious trustee of public powers, an enlightened, practical friend of
business methods and civil service reform
principles, and a promoter of appointment
and selection by merit, of tenure during com-
petency and good conduct, and of promotion
for cause.

The news columns of this paper to-day
outline the facts of his life. They involve
too many details to need recapitulation here.
Here we would but recall the spirit of the man

who has gone. That spirit was consecration
to duty without saying anything about it. It
was devotion to ideals without the preachment
of them. His was a life in the fear of God
without protrusion of the fact, and in the love
of man without proclamation of the feeling.
From the merely ordinary impression which
he casually made on casual acquaintances one
grew to realize by friendship and association
the sterling qualities of his character, the
thoroughness of his knowledge, the clearness
of his judgment, the fineness of his tastes, the
completeness of his faith in the people, the
deep and rational nature of his confidence in
free institutions, the abiding sense of his soul
in the things which are not seen and which
are eternal, and the tenacity — indeed, if need
were supplied, the heroism — of his moral
courage for that which he regarded as right.

His was solidity without showiness. His
was earnestness without the manner of it. His
was sincerity of action without the advertise-
ment of demonstrativeness. Had the gift of
magnetism or the art of eloquence or the in-
stinct of demagogy or the love of popularity,

or any of those things which lead a man to
exploit himself, while living himself, been his,
John B. Woodward would have been more
quickly understood, yet more readily dismissed, more promptly appraised, yet more
rapidly discounted.   We sometimes wished
that his modesty or indifference to effects did
not make him, so to speak, stand in his own
light.   Yet we soon got over that feeling, because we realized that although the divine
qualities in him were not dramatic, they were
real, and perhaps because not dramatic they
were the more real.

Not one of the men whose character and
position make them known to Brooklyn as the
exponents of her life, the custodians of her
confidence, the trustees of her purposes, and
the forthspeakers of her will, will fail to feel
that a noble colleague and an honored leader
has gone from them to-day.   Not one of them
will be able at once calmly to express or
rightly to estimate the loss which the city has
sustained in his death.   Not one of them was
prepared for the news of his decease, since all
of the inferences from his good health in later

years, and from the simplicity and wholesome-
ness of his habits his whole life through,
kindled confidence in the ability of his constitution to repel the attack upon the citadel
of his strength. To-day the words must be
words rather of record than of review, words
of sorrow rather than of measurement, words
of the heart rather than words of history.

We do know, however, that while citizenship is less by his loss it will be more because
of his example. We do know that while learning will number another of its benefactors
among the dead, its surviving friends will
draw inspiration and dedication from the
precious legacy of the immortal spirit of this
man of manifold unsuspected services to the
advance of humanity on the lines of better
living and of nobler laws. We know that
pure religion and undefiled will be more here,
and in circles hence widening out afar, because of the influence upon toleration, upon
reverence, and upon love, of this man, some of
whose creed was in every church and all of it
in none. We tender to his stricken kindred a
profound and respectful condolence. We as-

sure the representatives of the great moral,
humane, and educational causes which he
served of Brooklyn's sense of participation in
the loss which they have sustained. And we
would say to partizans in all camps of opinion
here that the study of this career and the sincere imitation of this life, which passed from
action into the silences to-day, involve one of
the truest lessons which they can pursue, and
if the lesson be rightly learned it will yield
such a force and such a fruitage of good for
decades to come as will add to the best wealth
which Brooklyn has—her estate in the character of her best children.

On Sunday morning the Unitarian Church
of our Saviour, in Pierrepont Street, which
General Woodward had attended for many
years, and which his father helped to found,
was thronged, not only with the regular con-
gregation, but by a large number of persons
from all parts of the city who had been at-
tracted by the notice that the pastor, the Rev.
Samuel A. Eliot, would refer to General Woodward's death, in his sermon. He said, in part:

We are met under the shadow of a common sorrow. He who has so long been a pillar of strength among us, the friend and helper of all, is missed from his accustomed seat. We can hardly realize the fact as yet. Only last Sunday he broke with us here the communion bread. We still expect to see his tall figure filling the doorway. . . . God grant that such assurance may be ours to-day, so that our cries of mourning may be turned at last to prayers of gratitude for the life lived so long and so nobly with us, the life of geniality, kindly activities, and wide sympathies; the life of charitable judgment, of broad humanity, of simple, sincere, and unobserved piety. We cannot associate with death the thought of a man so warm with the affections and wise with the thoughts that take hold of immortal life. We cannot believe that that sunshine of life is stricken or interrupted. Its warmth and heat were perhaps less felt because the soul did not show us the contrast of chilliness. No defects gave prominence to the excellencies. Where there are no shadows it is hard to appreciate the brilliancy of the

25

light, but as I think of that broad, genial life
I know not how to paint the shadows. I have
known just men who were hard and severe,
and I have known humane men who were soft
and sentimental—rarely do we meet a man
in whose character justice and tenderness are
balanced. These days of competition tend to
create characters which are irregular, exagger-
ated, and with one good quality dwarfed in
another. Here was the harmonious development of all. He was not

> Great for an hour, heroic for a scene,
> Inert through all the common life between.

His character was singularly symmetrical.
His mind, heart, and conscience had no in-
direct and circuitous methods. He went
straight to his point by the most sunlit road
—a characteristic of brave and single-minded
natures. A simple dignity, a spontaneous
courtesy which disregarded all the artificial
distinctions of society, marked all his intercourse with his fellow-men. For years past
there has hardly been an important institution
or enterprise which has proved to be for the

real good of this community with which he
has not been influentially connected. In him
the good sense, the humane instincts, the
higher ambitions of this city were individual-
ized.

This is no time for studied panegyric, and
nothing would have been less to his taste.
Never was man more unconscious of the love
and honor he had freely won — but we who
were glad of his fellowship may in our grief
rejoice to remember the virtues which grew
with the growth and strengthened with the
strength, the posts of duty met and filled with
wisdom and fidelity, the good causes sustained
and guided with prompt and intelligent devotion, the years of successful industry in business life and of manly tenderness in domestic
relations. That path of public spirit and magnanimity has no ending. The heart that was
larger than his great frame knows no anni-
hilation. The virtues were such as have
honor in the presence of God, for the Father
needeth such to serve him. In the maturity
of his powers the earthly career of usefulness
has been suddenly arrested, yet is the message

to us still a message of abundant life. His
very going may have power to waken in our
minds a deep sense of the blessings we enjoy
in this Christian fellowship and of the obliga-
tion of public-spirited service and private
honor which rest upon us. He has left us the
inspiration of that which the grave cannot
enclose nor death itself disintegrate, the solid
substance of a firm-knit character. By our
outreaching love, by our unceasing diligence,
by our sincerity of faith, may we prove ourselves not unworthy of his friendship and not
unmoved by his example.

The death of General Woodward, his life,
his character, and his activities, furnished
themes for remark and eulogium in many
other pulpits.

The funeral services were conducted in the
Church of Our Saviour on Monday, the ninth
of March. The Board of Aldermen adjourned
and the Mayor and most of the city officials
attended the services. The church was completely filled. The Rev. Mr. Eliot again spoke,
his remarks being as follows:

I sometimes think that the worth of a man is justly measured by the character of the friends who mourn for him. That so large a representation of our best citizenship should be present here to-day is the well-deserved tribute of the city to the man in whom were incarnated the wisdom, the humane instincts, the public spirit of this community. We are here to testify to the influence which this man of simple, genial, upright life has had upon our hearts and upon our higher ambitions. His very physical presence inspired confidence, his dignity enforced respect, his cordial friendliness won our love. He always seemed to me to take life in a large way, unvexed by disappointments, sunning himself in the warmth of domestic affections, giving a wholesome energy to many noble enterprises, always less anxious to shine in the estimation of others than to preserve his own self-respect. His genuineness of nature revolted from all pretension, a mental integrity and a robust moral health ran through his whole being. He had the large, sober, manly common-sense and the kindly, generous heart that we Americans demand in the leaders that we trust and follow. The champion of many good causes, he escaped the narrowness that comes from exclusive devotion to a particular cause. His great human sympathies and manly devotion communicated themselves to all who served with him in any high enterprise, touching and unsealing the springs alike of resolution and magnanimity. Sweetness played about his force. There was always charity in his judgments and gentleness in his might. But his tenderness and toleration did not make him compliant. He was capable at once of righteous indignation against error and evil and of compassion toward the evil-doer. His Christianity was broad and practical. He stood on ground of duty and of conscience rather than of opinion. He did not seek to penetrate into the dark places of theology, but whatever good his hands found to do he did it with his might. Inheriting his allegiance to this house of God, he held with sincere and unobtrusive piety the simple form of Christian faith taught here. He loved it and he lived it. Finally, he had the kindling, animating power which we call soul, which comes from no extent of learning, no breadth of understanding, no depth of sentiment, but is the attribute of commanding personality alone. With or against our will we caught from him courage, patriotism, charity, confidence in principle and trust in God.

The Rev. Charles Cuthbert Hall, D. D., pastor of the First Presbyterian Church of Brooklyn, and a warm friend of General Woodward, also delivered an address. Some of his remarks are quoted:

Although this occasion is preëminently mournful, although what we see before us awakens most acutely our sense of an untimely death, there is yet, friends and brothers, an element of nobleness in this hour, a message of strength which is an inspiration to every earnest man. . . . The words I am now speaking are intended to express love and gratitude to one who has gained the one and has earned the other without knowing it. If the dead know the sentiment their lives have

inspired, then our friend knows to-day what
he little knew or dreamed of on earth. There
was a public man who had not sought publicity for his own sake, who became a public
man by necessity rather than by choice, became self-consecrated to the public good.
With all the courage of his convictions, the
virility of his will, the perseverance of his
work in fulfilling what he had undertaken, I
believe him to have been a man of humble
spirit, severe in judging himself, estimating at
the most modest valuation the work he did.
In the last hours of his life, that time when
men are not wont to dissemble their real
thoughts, there fell from him words that bore
pathetic witness to his humble estimate of
himself. In life he would have resented vain
laudation and would have doubted the sincerity of those that offered it. We do not offer it
to his memory, but as his most untimely death
sets before the community in the broad light
of fact and record the tenor of his life and the
fruits of his labors, it cannot be denied, and it
need not be concealed, that he has won our
love and that he has earned our gratitude.

The intellectual opportunities of this city have been broadened and its intellectual reputation has been extended by his vigorous leadership of a great public movement in this direction. The true civic spirit and the true national spirit in himself has fanned in many, and has kindled in some, a like spirit. He dies rich in friends who cannot let his bodily presence vanish from them without saying over his grave these words of free-hearted love and honest appreciation.

After the services the body was interred in the General's plot in Dell Avenue, Greenwood Cemetery.

IX

TESTIMONIALS OF MANY ASSOCIATIONS

AT the time of General Woodward's decease he was President of the Brooklyn Art Association, President of the Thomas Jefferson Association of Brooklyn, and President of the Shore Road Commission. He was Vice-President of the Third National Bank of New York, Vice-President of the Brooklyn Institute of Arts and Sciences, and Vice-President of the National Rifle Association. He was Treasurer of the Commercial Mutual Insurance Company and Treasurer of the Birkbeck Investment Savings & Loan Company of America. He was a Director in the Atlantic Mutual Insurance Company, in the Franklin Trust Company, in the Franklin Safe Deposit Company, in the American Saw Company, in the Beckett Foundry & Machine Company, and in the Brooklyn Homeopathic Hospital.

He was a member of the New York Chamber
of Commerce, the New York Maritime Associa-
tion, the Down Town Association, the Society
of Old Brooklynites, the Brooklyn Club, the
Hamilton Club of Brooklyn, the Brooklyn
Riding & Driving Club, the Rembrandt Club,
the American Yacht Club, the Laurentian
Club, the American Association for the Advancement of Science, Commonwealth Lodge
No. 409 Free and Accepted Masons, Phœnix
Chapter No. 2 Royal Arch Masons, the Grand
Army of the Republic, the Loyal Legion, and
he was an honorary member of the American
Association of Public Accountants, of one of
the oldest lodges of Masons in New York, of
the Thirteenth Regiment Veteran Association,
of the Veteran Association Brooklyn City
Guard, G Company, Twenty-third Regiment,
and of several other associations. Most of
those bodies met and adopted memorials
expressive of the sentiments and emotions
occasioned by his death. The testimonial of
the Brooklyn Institute of Arts and Sciences
was reported by a committee composed of
the Rev. Richard S. Storrs, D.D., Carll H. De

Silver, A. Augustus Healy, the Rev. Charles
R. Baker, D.D., C. L. Woodbridge, the Hon.
Felix Campbell, and Professor Franklin W.
Hooper. It declared the loss of General
Woodward to be "as unexpected as it is im-
measurable." It recited the facts of his long
and intimate association with the Institute,
and said, "General Woodward was fully cog-
nizant of the plans of each and every department of the Institute's work, and followed
the details of their organizations with untiring
faithfulness and with the deepest interest. He
was a frequent attendant upon their lectures
and meetings, presiding at most of the important gatherings held under the auspices of the
Institute, constant in his attendance at the
meetings of the Board of Trustees and of its
several committees, and a wise counselor in
each and every matter that pertained to the
Institute's interests. His great experience in
public affairs, his wide acquaintance with the
citizens of the city and of the State, together
with his natural organizing power and executive ability, his great prudence and foresight,
made his services as President of the Institute

and as a member of the Board of Trustees of
wholly unequaled value. His open, frank,
and generous disposition, his lovable and
beautiful character, won for him and for the
Institute over which he presided, success in
everything that he undertook. General Woodward bound to himself by his rare and admirable personal qualities the love and esteem of
all the members of this Board, as well as of all
his fellow-citizens who had the honor and
pleasure of his acquaintance and the inspiration of his example, and this Board has lost,
in his death, a personal friend most dear to
each of its members, a servant most faithful
to the interests of the Institute, while the city
and nation have lost a most valuable citizen, a
brave soldier, a beloved and honored patriot."

A memorial meeting in honor of General
Woodward was held in the Church of Our
Saviour, under the auspices of the Brooklyn
Institute, on Thursday evening, the seventh
of May, 1896. The edifice was once more
filled with men and women sensible of their
loss and desirous of showing their respect for

the memory of their friend.   The following
order of exercises was observed:

Organ Voluntary.
Prayer,   The REV. J. C. AGER.
Hymn,   "Dear Refuge of My Soul,"   BAUMAN.
Opening Address,   PRESIDENT A. AUGUSTUS HEALY.
Memorial Address,   The REV. SAMUEL A. ELIOT.
Memorial Ode,   The REV. JOHN W. CHADWICK.
Hymn, "On High the Stars Brightly Shining",

RHEINBERGER.
General Woodward as a Citizen,
        Address by GENERAL STEWART L. WOODFORD.
General Woodward as a Soldier,
        Address by the HON. WM. H. BULKELEY.
Hymn, "Christian Warrior See Him Stand."
Benediction,   The REV. SAMUEL A. ELIOT.

A complete report of the meeting was published in a volume by the Institute.

Other expressions were equally appreciative
and valued.   The Hon. Joseph C. Hendrix,
President of the Brooklyn Club, addressing
Mrs. Woodward, said, "On behalf of the members of this club who were honored by the
friendship of your distinguished husband I
beg to express to you their sincere sorrow and

their genuine sympathy with you and your family. We all loved your noble husband. He was dear to us. We shall miss him." The secretary of Commonwealth Lodge F. & A. M. wrote, on behalf of that lodge, "His life was governed by the highest standard of humanity. Generous in all things, large-hearted and open-handed, patient in endurance of suffering, faithful to the last hour of his life in the performance of duty, he leaves a record which forms a bright example to all and a memory which all the members of this Lodge will cherish, happy that they have been permitted to call such a man by the sacred name of brother." The directors of the American Saw Company, of which General Woodward was at one time president, said, "His connection with the company extended over twenty-five years, and his wise counsel has been of invaluable service in the management of its affairs. His absence will be generally felt in the work of the company and at our meetings, and it is with a sense of personal loss that we recall his strong and kindly nature and his frank and genial manner, which have endeared him to us all."

The minute adopted by the Board of Trustees of the Commercial Mutual Insurance Company, of which General Woodward had been a trustee for about twenty-five years, contained the following expressions: "He was a man among men, a man of rank everywhere, of simple habits, approachable to all, gentle and kind to a marked degree, unassuming in manner and unostentatious in life, overflowing with good humor, and a choice companion to such as chanced to be intimate with him. . . . . Few men have done more in our time for the great public without compensation than he. . . . He was a model citizen in this respect. Physically he was a man of stalwart proportions, while mentally he measured up to the same high standard. . . . His advice was much sought by all who knew him." The Board of Trustees of the Atlantic Mutual Insurance Company referred to his "high business honor" and his "strong and positive convictions, with his faithfulness in the discharge of duty." The resolutions of the Board of Trustees of the Franklin Trust Company of Brooklyn mentioned that "General Woodward was an original member of this Board, was always faithful in his attendance at its meetings as well as in committees, and . . . aided the administration of the company in every way possible, and sincerely endeared himself to us all." The Board of Directors of the Third National Bank of New York declared that the members had "through a long series of years of intimate business relationship learned to honor our deceased associate as a wise and prudent counsellor, a faithful friend, and a citizen of the highest type, whose most earnest purpose in life was the advancement of his fellow-men"; they referred to his "calmness of judgment, his geniality of manner, and his sincerity of purpose in all things," and added that he "had endeared himself to us to a degree far transcending ordinary business friendships." The Maritime Association of the Port of New York in its testimonial stated that the members "have lost a faithful and efficient Auditor, whom they have unanimously elected for eight consecutive years," and spoke of his "unsullied record." The trustees of the Birkbeck

27

Company recalled that "he was one of the
organizers of this association, and ever since
its institution has shown the most cordial interest in its welfare, serving as its Treasurer
with rare efficiency and without remuneration,
and as a member of its directory giving un-
stintedly of his time and priceless experience,
actuated solely by a desire to be of value and
assistance to his fellow-men."

The Trustees of the Brooklyn Homeopathic
Hospital, in the minutes adopted by them,
said that in the death of General Woodward
the hospital "has lost one of its oldest and
most honored members. He has served the
institution in many capacities, continuously
since its formation in 1871. Never in all its
history has he failed in the discharge of any
duty he was called upon to perform. Not only
has he given generously to its support, but he
has also given freely the wisest counsel, which
in certain vicissitudes was of supreme value.
Among the traits of his character which were
always conspicuous were his manliness and
uprightness, which sympathized with and re-
sponded to every sentiment which was noble,

straightforward, and true, and despised every
word and deed that was false, base, and small;
his loyalty to every friend and his devotion to
every cause which he espoused, and the abso-
lute fidelity with which he discharged every
duty large and small. . . . He was always gentle, modest, considerate, and kind; his advice
was always ready, but it was given with respect for the opinions of others. His noble
presence, his winning personality, his ripe experience, and his wise counsel will be missed
in many circles in this city, but in no place
will they be more missed and deplored than in
the hospital with which he served so faithfully
for twenty-five years." The staff of the hospital also adopted resolutions expressive of
their sense of the "great loss to the hospital
and the community."

From the memorial of the Rembrandt Club
the following expression is taken: "In the
death of General John B. Woodward the Rembrandt Club has lost one of its most devoted
friends and supporters, its members a most
courteous and unselfish associate, and the
community a citizen conspicuous for benevo-

lence and approved ability, unaffected modesty, and wise public spirit." The testimonial of the Brooklyn Art Association summarized the record of the General's work for the Association. It said, in part: "On the establishment of the Brooklyn Art School in connection with the Brooklyn Art Association he contributed generously to the funds required for the school, and was interested in its work and prosperity until the time of his death; he assisted many young artists to secure the advantages of better instruction in art schools in this city and abroad; and some of the most distinguished painters and sculptors of our country are indebted to him for such aid and encouragement as enabled them to take high rank in their professions. General Woodward was largely instrumental in completing those arrangements whereby about one third of the stock of the Art Association was purchased by the Brooklyn Institute of Arts and Sciences and the property of the Art Association thereby preserved for all time for use in carrying out the purposes of the incorporation of the Association."

Adjutant-General E. A. McAlpin in general orders announced the death of General Woodward, by order of the commander-in-chief of the National Guard of the State. General Orders No. 2, issued by Assistant Adjutant-General John B. Frothingham, by command of Brigadier-General McLeer, referred to General Woodward as "an ideal soldier of the National Guard," and said, "A military escort for the funeral suitable to his rank was tendered, but while the family appreciated the offer their preference was expressed that the burial should be in keeping with his conduct in life, that of the plain, unassuming, modest citizen."

The following expressions are from the preamble and resolutions of Rankin Post No. 10, Grand Army of the Republic. They mention the General "who for more than twenty-five years was a member of this Post, whose friendly and sympathetic interest in its welfare, in every way willing to assist in the objects of our order, and whose loyalty and charity were always manifested whenever the call was made on him," and add, "By the unstinted commendation as a citizen of this city, which came from all its best citizenship, we his comrades do rejoice that his name is found on the roster of Rankin Post and that we have felt the touch of his comradeship, and in death his memory to us shall still be precious." The tribute of the Commandery of the State of New York, Military Order of the Loyal Legion of the United States, refers to General Woodward as "one of its earliest and most distinguished members." It recites many of the chief events of his life and summarizes some of his characteristics, and concluding, says: "He was a Christian gentleman. . . . He was manly and honest, he hated a lie, and he despised all shams. He was as loyal to the city and the State in civil affairs as he was true to his country in its time of trouble. . . . To those who knew him no record is needed to keep alive the memory of this rare man, one of nature's noblemen, grand and irreproachable."

The preamble and resolutions adopted by the "John B. Woodward Guard, Company E, Fourteenth Regiment, N. G. S. N. Y.," refer to the General "whose name our company has carried for over twenty-three years, and whose counsel and advice have often assisted us, making more plain our duties, responsibilities, and obligations to our country, as guardsmen." Part of the preamble is quoted: "The severance of the close bonds that attached us to him during his lifetime are now replaced by a memory which we shall cherish and transmit to our future comrades as emblematical of all that is truest and best in the career of a soldier. From private to major-general step by step he rose, honored by our State, trusted by our city, and in each call made upon him still further increasing our confidence and regard." The resolution of Company G, Twenty-third Regiment, formerly the "Brooklyn City Guard," contained, with much else of an affectionate and laudatory character, the following expressions: "On the long roll of honor of men who began their military service in our ranks no name shines so brightly, none meant so much to us, as that of John B. Woodward. No set form of words can tell our sorrow, no high-sound-

ing phrases for younger eyes that shall read
this in years to come could preserve to them
the sweetness of his memory. . . . His high
distinction was in no part due to self-seeking.
It was the inherent nobleness of his character
that made men honor him. His giant frame
was but the tenement of a great heart. His
was goodness without condescension, strength
without violence, nobility without pride. He
was tender to the faults of others, yet never
weak; he was firm yet never obstinate; he always spoke the truth, yet never wounded the
feelings of any; and when all is said it only
echoes this—we shall not look upon his like
again." The Veteran Association of the
Brooklyn City Guard said, "With our company he was first identified, more than forty
years ago and ever since, and in our meetings
and social gatherings he was a leader whose
conduct, discretion, and apt words imparted
life to the festivities and a charm to our annual reunions." Among the expressions in
the resolutions of the Thirteenth Regiment
Veteran Association are these: "A vacancy
has been made which no closing up of ranks

can fill. . . . In the man we recognized honesty and ability; in the friend we felt sympathy and sincerity; in the commander we acknowledged justice and guidance; and in the comrade we knew the love and fellowship of a noble heart."

The minute of the Shore Road Commission said, " . . . General Woodward's public spirit, pure motives, singleness of purpose, admirable disposition, exceptional discretion, conciliatory manner, and abundant energy, that enabled him to coöperate in so many movements for improving the city and ameliorating the conditions of life within its borders, made him in recent years the most useful citizen of Brooklyn. Future generations must be made aware of their obligations for his services in promoting the progress of the Shore Road, but only his associates in this commission can fully appreciate the value of his leadership in this splendid enterprise."

X

HOME LIFE—COMMEMORATIVE STATUE

THE time General Woodward gave to the
causes that have been named, and to
many others that are unrecorded, was not
taken from his family. His home life was one
of perfect happiness. In 1870, on the thirty-
first of May, his birthday anniversary, he was
married to Elizabeth Cook Blackburne, daughter of Robins Cook Blackburne. About eighteen months afterward he bought the house
at No. 259 Henry Street, Brooklyn. Here three
of his four children were born. Here one of
them, a boy ten years old, died, and exactly
three years afterward a daughter, aged sixteen, bereavements from which, notwithstanding his native cheerfulness, he never quite recovered. And here his wife, his oldest son,
Robins Blackburne Woodward, and his oldest daughter, Mary Blackburne Woodward,

215

watched by his side while his noble life ebbed away. Except for these children, their coming and their going, the General's married life was uneventful and contented. Nothing can testify so well of this important matter as his will, which was written by himself, and is appended:

"I, John B. Woodward, of the city of Brooklyn, New York, do make, publish, and declare my last will and testament as follows: I give, devise, and bequeath all the property and estate, whether real, personal, or mixed, wherever the same may be situated, of which I may be possessed or in any way entitled, absolutely in fee simple without any conditions, limitations, or exceptions whatever, to my wife Elizabeth C. Woodward and to her heirs and assigns forever. She has been a true, faithful, and devoted wife and mother. I confide all my property to her, knowing full well that she will use it for the benefit of our children more than I should be willing to ask her to do. I constitute and appoint my said wife sole executrix of this will, and it is my desire that she shall not be required to give any bond or security for the discharge of her duty as such.

"In testimony whereof I hereto sign my name, this tenth day of March, 1893.

"JOHN B. WOODWARD."

With this touching and characteristic tribute this volume might appropriately end, but one thing more deserves to be mentioned. The first shock of surprise at the announcement of General Woodward's death had scarcely passed when from many quarters arose expressions of a feeling that there ought to be some lasting monument of this peerless man. In the evening of the day of his burial a number of men who knew his worth met at the Hamilton Club to discuss the subject, and there and then formed a provisional organization for carrying the business forward. It was then stated that when General Woodward was in Paris, the year before, when he made his long journey to South America, his young friend the sculptor MacMonnies had persuaded the General to allow a cast to be made of his head. The knowledge of this fortunate act at once determined the general character of the monument, and a sub-committee was appointed to immediately apprise Mr. MacMonnies of the desire of the General's fellow-townsmen for a statue of some sort. The Hon. Frederick W. Wurster, who at that time was Mayor of the city, entered heartily into the project and invited a large number of citizens to meet at the City Hall to devise ways and means for effecting the purpose described. At this meeting it was resolved to erect such a monument as had been contemplated, and an executive committee was appointed for the more convenient transaction of the business. Subscriptions were invited, and the sum of fifteen thousand dollars, which was mentioned as essential to the suitable carrying out of the design, was quickly subscribed by a large number of persons. There were those who suggested that the statue should stand in Prospect Park, of which General Woodward was so fond, and which he had done so much to preserve and improve. It was also urged that it would be felicitous to put the bronze memorial on some well-chosen spot along the

Shore Road with which his name is indissolu-
ably associated. But at this time it seems to
have been finally and with almost universal
approval decided that General Woodward's
statue ought to stand in close association
with the great museum building of the Brooklyn Institute, itself a magnificent monument
that recalls his wisdom and foresight, his tact
and perseverance, and his extraordinary services for the education and refinement of the
people of his native city.